W9-AQK-784

THE FEATHERED SOMBRERO

THE FEATHERED SOMBRERO

NORMAN A. FOX

Thorndike Press • Chivers Press
Thorndike, Maine USA Bath, England

This Large Print edition is published by Thorndike Press, USA and by Chivers Press, England.

Published in 1997 in the U.S. by arrangement with Richard C. Fox.

Published in 1997 in the U.K. by arrangement with Golden West Literary Agency.

U.S. Hardcover 0-7862-1080-X (Western Series Edition)
U.K. Hardcover 0-7540-3020-2 (Chivers Large Print)
U.K. Softcover 0-7540-3021-0 (Camden Large Print)

Thorndike Large Print ® Western Series.

The text of this Large Print edition is unabridged. Other aspects of the book may vary from the original edition.

Set in 16 pt. Plantin by Rick Gundberg.

Printed in the United States on permanent paper.

British Library Cataloguing in Publication Data available

Library of Congress Cataloging in Publication Data

Fox, Norman A., 1911–1960.
The feathered sombrero / Norman A. Fox.
p. cm.
ISBN 0-7862-1080-X (lg. print : hc)
1. Large type books. I. Title.
[PS3511.O968F43 1997]
813′.54—dc21 97-335

CONTENTS

CHAPTER I

GUNS AT HALFWAY HOUSE

An ill wind blew Rowdy Dow and Stumpy Grampis into the night-blackened Bearclaw country, a cantankerous wind, blind to calendars and oblivious to common sense; for this was late spring, and the wind had made up its mind that it was still winter. It had an ambition, that wind — it was going to blow up a snowstorm or know the reason why! It howled through the pine-clad hills like a goosed banshee; it brought a scud of stinging rain with it, and conducted itself in sundry other ill-mannered ways, threatening to wrench the sombreros from the partners' heads or to rip the buttons from their slickers.

Yet, in all fairness to the wind, it wasn't entirely responsible for the present misery of that trouble-shooting pair, Rowdy and Stumpy. Certainly it hadn't been the wind that had placed an advertisement in the personal columns of a Miles City newspaper — an advertisement that had fetched the partners halfway across Montana to the mountainous Bearclaw country where the seasons were as scrambled as a Siwash song. The advertisement had said: "Rowdy Dow. If you are interested in a well-paying, adventurous assignment, write Captain Buck Trimble, care of Rancho Del Diablo, Bearclaw, and tell me you are coming. I will find you in Bearclaw and you will recognise me by a feathered sombrero I shall be wearing."

No more than that.

The advertisement, Rowdy had learned, had appeared intermittently in the paper since the previous fall, not many months after Rowdy, erstwhile outlaw of note, had been pardoned by a harassed governor. But Rowdy and Stumpy had roundsided through the winter with no other literature than a mail-order catalogue, and, of late, they had been occupied in the badlands along the Missouri. Thus it was only recently that the advertisement had been brought to their attention.

Whereupon Rowdy had made certain inquiries about Captain Buck Trimble, sent a short note to the man, and taken the trail to Bearclaw, the reluctant Stumpy in tow. Their activities in the badlands had been lucrative enough to leave them a comfortable bank balance in Miles City, and Stumpy had had peaceable plans involving poker and whisky. Now he sat a wet saddle many miles from nowhere and cursed.

A little man, Stumpy, with half a century and more of vicarious living behind him, he was leathery and grizzled and had a sprinkling of frost in his thinning hair and down-tilted moustache. He had heard the owl hoot, but his likeness had never adorned a reward dodger, and his greatest claim to fame was a sulphuric vocabulary which had been known to sour buttermilk. With the trail widening so the two could ride stirrup to stirrup, he unleashed a litany of profanity that made their horses blush. Mostly it had to do with Captain Trimble and the addle-headedness of Rowdy Dow who'd been enticed from comfort by Trimble's request. But as he grew spent of breath, Stumpy voiced a plea.

"That feller that give us directions on the other side of the hill spoke of a place called Halfway House," Stumpy recalled. "We must be gittin' near it. Why don't we put up for the night, Rowdy? Bearclaw town ain't gonna move meanwhile."

To this, Rowdy Row turned a disarming, cherubic smile. His was a choir-boy's face, the epitome of innocence, and his other attributes, as recently described on reward dodgers, were a mop of black hair, inclined to curl, and a formidable body which tipped the beam at a hundred and seventy. Twenty-eight years old, he was given to the wearing of bench-made boots, foxed trousers and pearl-buttoned shirts.

"The fellow who directed us likewise said we could reach Bearclaw by daylight," he remarked. "We haven't lost anybody at Halfway House. The thing that interested you, old horse, was that the jigger said Halfway House had a bar."

"These hills is likely teeming with liars," Stumpy argued. "Living on slopes onsettles people's brains. I'll betcha Bearclaw is two, three days' ride from here."

"No!" Rowdy said firmly, knowing his partner's weakness for anything alcoholic. "Nothing doing."

"But I just *got* to celebrate to-night," Stumpy insisted, shouting above the wind. "This here night comes but once a year."

"Your birthday," Rowdy reminded him, "is either a long ways past or a long time coming, whichever way you look at it."

"It ain't that," Stumpy said. "Till midnight it's Uncle Tio's day. And it's only fitten and proper I celebrate it."

"Uncle Tio's day? Never heard of it."

"It all goes back to when I was a little gaffer," Stumpy explained. "I was being brought up in a town down on the Mexican border. This here town was set on the slope of a hill that used to be a volcano, but it hadn't erupted for more centuries than ten men could remember. And then one day a grey-whiskered *nativo* rode into the village on a burro and called all the folks together. He told us the volcano was going to kick up a fuss, and if we didn't move out pronto we'd all be up to our ears in lava!"

"Yeah?" said Rowdy.

"Well, some folks figgered this old Mex was crazy, but some, like my paw, believed him, and we moved out. And you can stake me out on an anthill with maple syrup poured all over me if that volcano didn't go BOOM! that very night! The only ones saved was us folks that listened to the old Mex. Uncle Tio, he called hisself. Us survivors has been scattered to the four corners of the earth, but, no matter where we are, when to-day rolls around, the anniversary of that day we was warned, we always hoist a couple in honour of Uncle Tio. But for him, Rowdy, I'd have been nothing but a cinder!"

Rowdy's horse shied violently, almost unseating him. "You see?" Rowdy said. "Even my horse knows that's the most gosh-awful lie he ever heard. Uncle Tio's Day!"

But it wasn't the fantastic windy Stumpy

Grampis had spun that had caused Rowdy's horse to jump. The rain had increased this last half-hour, lightning flickering weirdly across the night sky, and now, with the lightning flaring again, both men saw the shapeless figure in the trail. A man lay there, face down, and the two, dismounting and cupping matches in their hands, saw to their great surprise that he was a Mexican, the most resplendently dressed one they'd ever seen, though both had sojourned along the brimstone border more than once.

"This is what comes of talking about Uncle Tio," Rowdy observed. "We've just run into his nephew."

The Mexican was dressed as if for a fiesta; his *charro* jacket was silver-braided as were his wide-bottomed trousers of black velvet; his sash was red silk, his shirt was white silk. Turned over, he proved to have a young, handsome, olive-skinned face with the merest whisper of a black moustache. His hair, too, was black — thick, curly hair matted with blood.

"Grazed by a bullet," Rowdy judged. "Or clouted over the head. There's still life in him. Pick up his sombrero, Stumpy, and help me get him into my saddle."

It took the combined effort of the partners to mount the Mexican, Rowdy clinging behind the unconscious man and holding him in place. The horse, double-burdened, threatened to pitch both of them on their ears, but Rowdy applied a firm hand to the reins, and after a hectic time they moved on down the trail. The partners kept their eyes peeled for a stray horse; obviously this not-so-gay caballero had not flown to a remote mountain trail; but no horse was in evidence. The Mexican was still unconscious when a mile had unreeled, and Stumpy said triumphantly, "Now we've shore enough *got* to stop at Halfway House, Rowdy. This pore unfortunate victim of the vee-sissy-toods of fate has got to be bedded down pronto."

Rowdy nodded, having already come to the same conclusion, but his mind was occupied with wondering who this fellow was and how he'd come to be laid low. Montana had its share of Mexicans, but not as many as the states farther south. And most of the Mexicans to be found this many miles from their homeland were usually of the peon class. Don Unconscious was definitely not one who toiled with his hands. Captain Buck Trimble's spread, somewhere in this hill country, was known as Rancho Del Diablo — Ranch of the Devil in the tongue of manana land — and there might be some connection. But speculation was fruitless and the wind laughed at him.

They came within the hour to Halfway House, a huge, two-storied log building, ramshackle and listing to windward and dark as the inside of a black cat on a stormy night. They clattered into the clearing that was the yard; to the rear was a log barn, but the partners left their horses standing in the yard with reins trailing, placing the need of a human above the need of the animals on this occasion. Supporting the Mexican between them, they climbed to the low gallery fronting the mountain hostelry and thumped loudly upon the heavy door. After an interminable time, the door opened and a lantern flashed in their faces.

"Whatcha want?" a gruff voice demanded inhospitably.

"A bed for this gent," said Rowdy. "Lead the way to one."

The holder of the lantern, a thick-necked, bullet-headed individual, looking no brighter than the law allowed, moved back a pace, showing no surprise at this nocturnal intrusion. "Follow me," he said.

He led them across a bar-room which Stumpy eyed with open anticipation and to a stair that was almost as steep as a wall. Up the stairs, the lantern bobbed along a hallway, and, their shadows dancing wildly, the partners toted the Mexican. The proprietor of Halfway House hesitated before a closed door. "Occupied," he grunted, and moved back to a door he'd just passed. It gave to his touch and he ushered the trio into a room with a bed, a bureau, and a couple of chairs. While Rowdy and Stumpy laid the Mexican upon the blankets, the proprietor fumbled a kerosene lamp alight.

"Wouldn't happen to be a sawbones under the roof?" Rowdy asked.

"Nope," said Bullet-head. "Only got one other room rented to-night. Nearest doc's in Bearclaw, on down the trail."

"Fetch some hot water," Rowdy instructed. "We'll wash this caballero up. I think he's only scratched."

The proprietor obediently departed; Rowdy tugged at the Mexican's boots and got them off, and it was when Rowdy was placing the boots upon the floor that the Mexican opened his eyes. He gazed about him in visible astonishment, and Rowdy said, "Now just take it easy. You're with friends."

"Gracias," said the Mexican. And then, very clearly: "I, senors, am Don Sebastian Gregorio Jose de Ibarra y Alvarez."

"Imagine it!" said Rowdy. "It must tax

your strength just to pack that handle around." But the Mexican had lapsed into unconsciousness again. In due time the proprietor reappeared with a steaming pitcher, and Rowdy fell to washing the caked blood from Don Sebastian's head. A long gash was thus revealed, and Rowdy, ripping a pillowcase into strips, bandaged the wound. Then he stepped back, a worried frown on his cherubic face.

"I don't like this, Stumpy," he said. "Maybe he's just slipped from unconsciousness into sleep, but I think he should have a sawbones. Come along. We were headed for Bearclaw, anyway. We can send the doc back from there."

Stumpy's lips twitched with a protest; he glanced at the injured Mexican and changed his mind. Only when they were downstairs and crossing the bar-room to the door did Stumpy show any real rebellion against the destiny that was sending him out into the wind and the rain once again. "Uncle Tio —" he began plaintively, glancing at the row of bottles behind the bar.

"Don't mention that name!" Rowdy sternly admonished him. "Want us to find another unconscious Mexican out on the gallery?"

The proprietor followed them to the door.

To him Rowdy handed a gold piece, saying, "This should cover the cost of his room. Do what you can for him. We'll have a sawbones back here as soon as possible."

The huge door closed behind them. They stepped from the gallery's shelter out into the sleazy darkness, groping towards the darker outline of their waiting horses. A hand on his saddle-horn, Rowdy glanced up at the row of second-storey windows, seeing the one where lamplight now burned. And just then the lightning flared and he saw the girl.

Her face was pressed to the window next to Don Sebastian's room, and her face was beautiful, and her face was frantic with fear. It seemed to Rowdy in that split second of light in darkness that she beckoned urgently to him, yet he couldn't be sure. He only knew that he had seen the white face and the shimmering black hair that fell to her shoulders and that her eyes had beseeched something of him.

"Stumpy!" he ejaculated. "Did you see her?"

"See who?" Stumpy asked, glancing around him.

"The girl! Up there in the window. Wait till the lightning flares again!"

But when the lightning flashed, after an

endless time, the window was blank.

"Rowdy," his partner said suspiciously, "let me smell yore breath!"

"I tell you there was a girl up there! And in some kind of trouble. Stumpy, I'm going back inside. Wait here and keep your eyes peeled. If I'm not out in about fifteen minutes, come after me. I aim to get to the bottom of this."

He climbed the gallery steps again and, remembering the long time it had taken to arouse the proprietor before, he didn't bother with the door, which was undoubtedly barred on the inside. Instead, he stepped to a window near the door and tested the sash. It refused to yield to him, and, nameless desperation goading him, Rowdy dug his gun out from under his slicker, smashed the pane and crawled through.

Inside, he groped his way across the darkened bar-room. There was no sign of the proprietor or his lantern, and apparently the fellow was too far away to have been aroused by Rowdy's violent entry. Finding the stairs, Rowdy ascended to the upper hallway and began groping along.

Light showed under only one doorway — the doorway to Don Sebastian's room. The door beyond was the goal of Rowdy's seeking, or so he'd judged from his observation outside and the remembered remark of the proprietor about that room being occupied, and he was almost to this door when there was swift movement in the darkness. Someone careened against Rowdy; a gun boomed thunderously, the flash blinding him, the bullet buzzing past his ear.

He'd carried his own gun in his hand since using the forty-five to smash the window, and he struck out wildly with it and lunged forward, his arms wrapping around a man. For an instant they were clawing at each other, and then Rowdy's opponent wrenched himself free, leaving a coat button in Rowdy's hand. Rowdy fired a random shot, hoping to locate his adversary in the gun-flash — a wasted effort. For even as he shot, a gun-barrel clouted him alongside his head and his knees gave way beneath him and he was hard put to cling to consciousness.

He went down stunned, hearing a wild threshing in the hallway, not knowing whether one person or a dozen were moving in the darkness. The stairs echoed to a great clatter; somewhere in the building a gun boomed again. Rowdy shook his head and managed to get on hands and knees, but no strength was in him to rise. He was this way when he heard Stumpy frantically bellowing his name, and Stumpy came roaring up the stairs.

"Here!" Rowdy cried weakly.

"Hell's tuh pay!" Stumpy ejaculated, helping Rowdy to his feet.

"That man — or men?" Rowdy demanded. "Did you see them?"

"I come runnin' when I heard a shot," Stumpy said. "There's a back door to this shebang. It's wide open right now and flappin' in the wind. Somebody got out that way. How many I couldn't tell. I was just climbing in at that window you busted. I tell yuh hell's tuh pay! The proprietor's downstairs stretched out dead. He must 'a' been in the way of them jiggers when they was leaving."

Rowdy remembered the shot he'd heard after he'd been stunned and his adversary had departed. He felt the coat button in his hand and thrust it into his slicker pocket.

"The girl!" he ejaculated and lurched across the hall to the door he'd never reached. The door was now open. Groping into the room, he fumbled for a match and got it alight and lifted it high. This room was much like the adjacent one in which Don Sebastian had been bedded. It, too, had a bed and bureau and a couple of chairs, and the bed hadn't been slept in. But there was no girl there.

The match flared out. Rowdy quickly struck another and moved to the window from which the girl's face had been peering. Ancient dust lay deep along the sill, and in that dust was a message, traced, undoubtedly, by a finger. It read: FELICIA — DIABLO — HELP!

"Rancho Del Diablo!" Rowdy muttered aloud. "Trimble's layout."

"And Felicia's a Mex name, ain't it?" Stumpy added, peering over Rowdy's shoulder. "Rowdy, these woods is shore full of things Mexican."

"And I'm going to have a look at one of them right now," Rowdy said. "Maybe the ruckus aroused Don Sebastian. Maybe he heard enough to be able to tell us something of what went on. There was a girl here, that's sure. A girl who needed help. Somebody dragged her out, and I was in his way when he did it. He clouted me and shot the proprietor to clear his path. You're right, Stumpy. There was hell to pay."

They moved out of this room and to the next one, and wasting no time on ceremony, Rowdy put his hand to the door and lurched inside. The lamp the now-dead proprietor of Halfway House had lighted still burned upon the bureau, and in its glow Rowdy saw all there was to see. The wind howled beneath the eaves; the wind laughed, hugging its secret to itself. For Don Sebastian Gregorio Jose de Ibarra y Alvarez had vanished into thin air.

CHAPTER II

THE SHOOTIN' SOREHEADS

Bearclaw, viewed in the murky dawn through a slanting drizzle, had a bedraggled see-what-the-cat-dragged-in look to it. The trading centre of a sizeable section of mountain country once dedicated to mining and now devoted to the raising of cows, the town was as haphazard as a drunkard's dream. Possibly Paul Bunyan had strode along Bearclaw Gulch one day with a pocketful of log and frame structures and had not discovered until afterwards that he'd had a hole in his pocket. Bearclaw looked like that. A sullen stream brawled beside it, muttering and bickering constantly as though just daring somebody to talk back. The buildings, a good many of them saloons, were all shuttered when Rowdy and Stumpy rode in. It might have been a ghost-town except that any reasonably gregarious ghost would have expired of sheer loneliness from the looks of the place.

"Brrrr!" Stumpy said, shivering in his saddle, and his comment was an echo of Rowdy's own unvoiced reaction to Bearclaw.

They had come here from Halfway House through the last of the darkness; they had not tarried long at the mountain tavern after their examination of Don Sebastian's empty room. They had laid out the dead proprietor on his own bar and had a look around, and there were tracks. Too many tracks. Their own muddy boots had made many markings. The back door swung open, creaking indication of the route of departure of those who had fled while Rowdy lay stunned upstairs.

"We might as well ride on to Bearclaw," Rowdy had announced. "No use looking for wisps of hay in a stack of needles."

Stumpy offered no objection; the attraction Halfway House had first had for him had most definitely palled. "This here place has got a curse on it," he told Rowdy. "Maybe you'd better hold my hand till we're out of here, old hoss. I got to make sure you don't disappear, too."

And so they had come to Bearclaw, a mystified pair who'd done much looking over their shoulders these last long miles. Into town, they sought out a livery stable, and after much pounding at its door, aroused a grumbling hostler who took care of their horses and directed them to a hotel. There was only one. An ancient clerk, more asleep than awake, presided at the desk, and when Rowdy signed the register he took a look at a fly-specked calender pinned to the wall. "This is the twenty-first, isn't it?" he asked.

"All day to-day," said the clerk, laying a key on the desk. "Number seven. End of the hall. This floor. We got two rules. No spittin' at the ceiling or goin' to bed with your spurs on."

As they followed the hall to the indicated room, Rowdy said, "I told Trimble we should hit here about the twenty-first, the way I calculated."

They had been supplied with a sway-backed bed, a bureau that most obviously had once been a packing case, the inevitable pitcher and bowl, a rawhide-bottomed chair, and a wall mirror which made their faces look zigzagged. The only window gave them a vista of a gloomy stretch of alley. As one man they peeled off their boots and stretched themselves upon the bed; they were hungry as well as tired, but they would breakfast later. Likewise they would seek out the law and report the death at Halfway House.

Before he dozed off, Rowdy said, "Hope Trimble shows up pronto. I wrote our names good and plain on the register."

He was soon asleep, Stumpy snoring beside him; and sunlight streamed through the window and the rain was gone when he awoke. Yet it was not the sunlight that had awakened Rowdy; it was some faint, alien sound, and at first he couldn't locate it. Then he realised that someone was scratching at the window. Shaking Stumpy into wakefulness, Rowdy said, "Got to get up and let the cat in. Hear it?" He crossed to the window, Stumpy reaching for the gun he'd laid on the floor beside the bed, and when Rowdy hoisted the sash, a man framed himself beyond the window and hastily clambered through.

"By your leave," said this man. "I'm Captain Buck Trimble. You'll pardon my method of entrance. I had to risk the lobby to find out which room you had, but there was no use tempting fate. Bearclaw is a town of enemies."

"Jumpin' Jehosh-aphat!" Stumpy ejaculated.

For their visitor was a man to remember. Tall and lean to the point of emaciation, he had a bony, cadaverous face, bloodless and thin-lipped. He wore a rusty black suit, the trousers tucked into riding-boots, a white shirt and a black string tie, and, all in all, he looked like a first-class job of embalming.

But it was his sombrero that was holding the partners' eyes. A broad-brimmed Mexican sombrero, seldom seen this far north of the border, its cone-shaped crown was covered by intricately-woven feathers. The man doffed the sombrero, revealing a high dome of a forehead and a sweep of black hair combed straight back.

"Here," he said, "is the feathered sombrero which was to identify me. You'll find many who'll tell you I'm never seen without it. Though I'll admit that I discarded it before I ventured into the hotel lobby. You're Rowdy Dow?"

"Right as rain," Rowdy said, stamping into his boots.

"I once saw your picture on a reward dodger. You don't resemble it a great deal. And this, I presume, is your partner, Lumpy Stumpit."

"Stumpy Grampis," that worthy insisted in a firm voice.

"Have a chair," Rowdy said, toeing the only one forward. "Let's get down to business. You ran an advert, offering me a good-paying proposition. You got my letter or you wouldn't be here to-day. I did a little looking into your history, Captain. It wasn't hard. You've got quite a rep, even though few people have actually known you."

Mephistophelian eyebrows arched. "Indeed, Mr. Dow? Few men are granted the privilege of seeing themselves as others see them. And just what facts have you unearthed?"

"Your title comes from heading some shirt-tail army in a Mexican revolution," Rowdy amplified. "You were a soldier of fortune when you were younger. Later you settled on a big ranch overlapping the border. Part of it came from the old Quintera land grant; the rest was on the American side. Years ago you moved your ranch up here to Montana. You've got a lot of acres back in these hills, and you've got a six-strand barbed wire fence with padlocked gates wrapped around those acres. Rifle-toting riders patrol that wire night and day. Am I right, so far?"

The feathered sombrero placed on his head again, the man nodded. "True, I live in a guarded domain. I've expanded my holdings into an empire, and some of the ranchers I dispossessed were removed by legal means, some otherwise. My right-hand man, a lawyer named Gideon Turk, is versed in finding loopholes in haphazard land claims. With his help I've built up my range. That's why Bearclaw is dangerous for me. The men I've ousted have united in a loose organisation which they call the Shootin' Soreheads. They'd kill me on sight. Hence the guarded fence; behind it I'm a law unto myself. You've a right to know these things before you take employment with me. Ask any question you please."

"What's the idea of that feathered J. B.?" Stumpy demanded.

"A sound idea, Grumple. My vaqueros were brought with me from the border. They are known locally as Mexicans, and perhaps they are. It depends on your view-point. Thousands of the descendants of the ancient Aztecs still dwell in Mexico, many of pure Indian blood, who are able to trace their ancestry back to the time of the Montezumas. Learned men will tell you that nowhere in Mexico do the Indians still retain the religion, customs and traditions of the Aztecs; the Spanish priests were too thorough in destroying everything that remotely resembled paganism. Yet the Guaymis, a people of the mountain fastnesses of Panama, still call their high chief Montezuma, embrace a religion which is a modified form of sun-worship, and have in their own talk a great deal of the pure Nahuatl language, which was the Aztec tongue. So who can dispute me when I say that Aztecs do exist to-day and that my own vaqueros are Aztecs rather than Mexicans, such as we know them?"

"That don't explain the hat," Stumpy insisted doggedly.

"Aztec chiefs and priests wore feathered headdresses," the other went on patiently. "One of the greatest attainments of the Aztecs was their feather-work, which was magnificent. They maintained immense aviaries of bright-plumaged birds for the sole purpose of having constant supplies of feathers for their purposes. I had this feathered sombrero fashioned down in Mexico many years ago. You might call it a modern equivalent of an Aztec headdress. That it is a constant reminder to my Aztecs that I am the man in power goes without saying. They are a superstitious lot. You'll scoff, of course, but my vaqueros have stoutly maintained that they've actually seen Quetzalcoatl, the plumed serpent god of the Aztecs. Seen him here in Montana!"

"Look," Rowdy said with a poorly stifled yawn, "this is all mighty interesting, but I'm a practical man. How about that paying proposition?"

His visitor studied him for a reflective moment. "I know your reputation, too, Dow," he said. "You cut quite a swath as an outlaw, and you were pardoned for saving some ranchers from a burst dam. How have you found life since you've taken to riding the straight and narrow?"

"I've managed to keep busy," said Rowdy.

"But you might be induced to make use of certain talents which your — er — former occupation developed?"

"If you're asking me whether I want to risk losing my pardon, the answer is no."

"Supposing the job were in Mexico?"

"Doing what?"

"As you've probably gathered, I have an intense interest in things pertaining to the Aztecs. I have quite a collection of Aztec relics at Rancho Del Diablo, but I've long desired to possess a certain item which has been beyond my reach. You see, Dow, the Aztecs, so far as we know, were the only pre-Columbian Americans to use the sword as a weapon. The Aztec sword, or *maquahuitl,* bore little resemblance to a sword such as we know one. The museum in Mexico City has an ancient sword, one which they claim is the sword of the last Montezuma. I want that sword. It may appear to be a whim to you, but I am a wealthy man and able to gratify my whims. When I heard of you, it struck me you were a man capably equipped to journey to Mexico City and get that sword for me by any means that might be required. I'll pay handsomely. If you will accept the proposition, I'll give you a detailed description of the sword and its present whereabouts. What is your decision?"

Rowdy spent no time in reaching one. "Nothing doing," he said. "Mexico and this country have been getting along fairly well since that little war they had quite a spell back. I'd just as soon leave it that way."

"That's your final answer?"

"Final."

The visitor sighed, then dipped a long, bony hand into his inner coat pocket and produced a wallet. "I'm sorry you feel as you do," he said. "Naturally, all that has passed in this room will remain a secret between us. How much do I owe you for the trouble of coming here?"

"Not a cent," Rowdy said. "We enjoyed the ride. Didn't we, Stumpy?"

Stumpy, almost strangling, muttered something inarticulate and unenthusiastic, and Rowdy, crossing to the window, raised the sash again. "You'll want to leave the way you came, Captain Trimble. Maybe you'll be able to find somebody else who's willing to take a pasear to Mexico. We'll keep the secret."

The feathered sombrero was swept off, its owner bending in a quick bow. "A good day to you, Dow. And to you, too, Lumpit. Pleasant riding on your return journey."

He clambered nimbly through the window and was gone; and Stumpy let out a long snort compounded of both amazement and dismay. "What's got into you, Rowdy?" he demanded as the window was closed again. "That jigger would have paid us for sittin' wet saddles, and you wouldn't take the money! A wild-goose chase, that's what this has been!"

"Now just nail down your shirt-tail," Rowdy advised. "We've got to get some breakfast. Then we've some riding to do. I aim to see the inside of Rancho Del Diablo."

"You aim to go to Trimble's ranch?"

"That's the notion. Have you forgotten Felicia, the girl who left a message for help? I've a hunch we'll find her on the other side of that padlocked fence."

"Why didn't you ask Trimble about her?" Stumpy demanded. "Just to see whether he'd have jumped."

"He'd have jumped all right," Rowdy said. "Here, take a look." He picked his slicker from where he'd tossed it across the foot of the bed and, delving into a pocket, produced the button he'd torn from the coat of the man he'd struggled with in the dark hallway of Halfway House. "This came off the jigger who almost gunned me down last night," Rowdy explained. "It matches the buttons on the coat of our late visitor, Captain Buck Trimble. And one of his was missing. I noticed that right off. He's the gent who snatched Felicia last night."

Stumpy stared, a man stunned. "Then why didn't you pretend to string along with him on the Mexico proposition, Rowdy? Likely he'd have taken us out to his spread to give us the detail about that Injun sword he wants. That way we'd have got through the fence without having to buck a batch of rifle-totin' riders."

"Captain Trimble," said Rowdy, "never had any intention of letting us see the inside of Rancho Del Diablo. Not even from the first, when he put that notice in the paper. We were to meet him here in Bearclaw, remember? He could have told us to come to the padlocked gate and be let inside; instead he arranged to meet us in a town where a bunch of galoots called the Shootin' Soreheads are aching for his scalp. Why, Stumpy?"

"Why? Why? Why?" Stumpy wailed. "All we've run into so far is question marks. Rowdy, I'm thinkin' we're up to our ears in trouble again."

"It sounds like it," Rowdy agreed, for

there was the heavy tramp of many boots out in the hallway, and someone kicked lustily at the door, bursting it inward. A half-dozen men came boiling into the room — grim-faced men with guns in their hands.

"Where is he?" one demanded. "Where did he head from here?"

"Now, see here —" Rowdy began.

"Don't stall! One of the boys saw him hurrying down the alley. No mistaking that feathered hat he wears. Buck Trimble was here. Now talk, damn it!"

Rowdy shrugged in surrender. "I think," he said to Stumpy, "that we've just met up with the Shootin' Soreheads. And the sign says that we're not popular with them. Not a bit."

CHAPTER III

CABIN CALABOOSE

Now here were men with the look of having fed on cactus and barbed wire and grown lean on the fare. Clad in nondescript range garb, they were alike in that each wore a belted gun and a tremendous scowl, and, crowded into the room, they pocketed Rowdy and his partner and ran heavy hands over them in search of hideout weapons. The partners' guns were tossed to a corner, and the one who'd so far acted as spokesman for these Shootin' Soreheads said, "I told you to talk! Where did Trimble light out to? And what was his business with you? You're right about us being the Shootin' Soreheads. And you're likewise right about us not carin' a whoop for you!"

"And just who are *you?*" Rowdy demanded.

"Abel Karst is the name."

He was a big man, Karst, solid of body and solid of features, a shock of grey-tinged black hair showing beneath his sombrero. Perhaps his face had once been kind; adversity had grooved grimness into each leathery line, and his shoulders had a belligerent hunch to them. Sizing him up, Rowdy wondered if all the juice of justice had been wrung out of that massive carcass and took a chance that a drop or two remained. "We could be a couple of saddle-tramps riding through," Rowdy said. "I don't see any badge sticking out on you. And I don't figure I have to answer your blasted questions."

"A lot of us hereabouts lost our ranches when Buck Trimble started dragging long spurs through these hills. Oh, it was legal enough in most cases — that son of a snake, Gideon Turk, saw to that. Them with families had to move on and find other acreage. But us galoots that was single stuck around. We make a dollar one way or another, and we give Rancho Del Diablo all the trouble we can fork out. Trimble is the law inside his barbed wire. We're the law here in Bearclaw. Without badges."

"Show 'em the inside of our jail-house, Abel," one of his companions spoke up. "Maybe that'll l'arn 'em we ain't bluffing!"

But Abel Karst waved a hand. "They've got a fair shake coming," he said. "They get a chance to clear themselves. We saw your names on the register. We've heard of you, Rowdy Dow. I even seen your picture once.

A helluva picture it was! We've laid our cards on the table. Trot yours out. What was Buck Trimble doing here?"

Rowdy yawned widely. "Maybe you're all wrong. Maybe he wasn't in this room."

A man came hurrying down the hall — another lean, sullen man. He burst into the room and singled out Karst and thrust a newspaper at him. "I went to the livery stable like you told me, Abel," he said. "Look what I found in the saddlebag of one of these strangers. This newspaper! Look at the notice that's been marked with a pencil!"

Karst, keeping his gun in his right hand, took the paper with the other and read aloud: "Rowdy Dow. If you are interested in a well-paying, adventurous assignment, write Captain Buck Trimble, care of Rancho Del Diablo, Bearclaw, and tell me you are coming. I will find you in Bearclaw and you will recognise me by a feathered sombrero I shall be wearing."

Stumpy had the horrified look of a man who has just found a scorpion in his pocket. "Now the fat's in the fire for sure!" he wailed.

Tossing the paper angrily to the floor, Karst's scowl turned blacker than a tar-papered thundercloud. "Bluffin', eh?" he snarled. "You *did* have business with Trimble! We couldn't be sure. We were runnin' a sandy ourselves. All one of our boys saw was that damn' feathered hat bobbin' down the alley *behind* this hotel. He wasn't even close enough to take a shot at Trimble. But when he told us about it, we came here and checked to see who Trimble might have been visitin'. There was only two strangers registered — you two! Now we've got proof you came here to meet Trimble. Talk, mister!"

"Trimble was here," Rowdy wearily admitted. "What he talked about is a secret. I can tell you this much — it didn't have a blasted thing to do with you boys."

Karst prodded Rowdy's ribs with his six-shooter. "Come along!" Karst ordered. "We're going to jug you two. We're going to keep you locked up till you spill the truth!"

Again Rowdy shrugged in surrender, knowing the futility of arguing with a gun. He and Stumpy were herded out of the room and along the hall to the lobby. The ancient clerk was no longer on duty; he had been replaced by an anæmic-looking, watery-eyed youth who stared in horror as the two prisoners were taken out to the street. With the sun shining and the weather at last caught up with the calendar, Bearclaw had a less bedraggled look to it, but Rowdy viewed the town with a jaundiced eye as they were hustled along the planking toward the outskirts where a log structure with a barred window loomed.

This building, its door held by a heavy padlock which Karst unlocked, proved to have a single room with a cot, a stool, and little else to furnish it. Shoved inside this cell, Rowdy and Stumpy contemplated it with disdain, Stumpy openly opining that he'd seen better jails.

Karst said, "When you feel like talking, poke your head between the bars of one of the windows and holler. Sooner or later we'll hear you."

"We haven't eaten yet to-day," said Rowdy. "You aim on starving us to death?"

"We'll fetch you grub," Karst promised, and the door was swung shut and padlocked.

Instantly Stumpy went to one of the windows, testing the bars, but they were firmly embedded in a wooden frame and didn't so much as quiver when Stumpy put his hands to them. Turning, he said, "Rowdy, we got to tell those Sorehead galoots the truth about Trimble. We don't owe him nothing, and keepin' his secret will mean stayin' in this calaboose the rest of our natural days.

Yeah, and our natural nights, too!"

"Too late," said Rowdy with a sigh. "Likely I shouldn't have tried bluffing in the first place, but I figured it might work. You've seen Karst and those others. How hard do you think they'd listen to a yarn about Trimble wanting us to take a pasear to Mexico City to steal an old sword? We could tell them a hundred lies that might sound sensible, but the truth is something we're just stuck with. They'd figure it was a bigger windy than that one you spun about Uncle Tio."

"A fine state the world's gittin' into," Stumpy snorted, "when truth, crushed to earth, is just so much fertiliser!"

Karst himself returned with a breakfast tray, edging into the room with a tray on one arm and a gun held in his free hand. He set the tray upon the stool and stepped back and even grinned faintly as the partners dived at it. Pouching his gun but keeping a safe distance from the two, Karst put his back to the log wall and shaped up a cigarette. The smoke going, he said, "We ain't meaning to be too harsh. If you'd bucked Rancho Del Diablo the way we've bucked it, you'd be leery, too."

Rowdy, his mouth full, managed to say, "We're stuck with that story about Trimble wanting us on a deal that hadn't anything to do with you boys."

Karst's scowl returned. "We can't take chances," he said. "It's war to the death between us and Buck Trimble. If we let you go, it might mean that pretty soon you'll be inside that fence workin' for Trimble. The paper said he had a proposition for you. Some day we're going to find our way through that padlocked gate. We'll have enough guns against us when that happens. Those Mex vaqueros of Trimble's can shoot. So can Gideon Turk, and that kill-crazy segundo, the Gopher Kid, who ramrods Trimble's crew. Maybe Trimble aimed on hiring more guns. As long as you're locked up here, that makes two less against us."

"Could you send one of your boys to the gate of Rancho Del Diablo under a flag of truce? Would you believe Buck Trimble if he sent back word that the proposition he offered me was turned down?"

"I wouldn't take Buck Trimble's word that it was raining," said Abel Karst, "if the water was running down my neck. And he wouldn't honour a flag of truce if one of our boys was packin' it. Likely our man would get shot out of his saddle."

Rowdy sighed. "We're getting no place so

fast we'll likely meet ourselves coming back."

Karst departed with the tray, padlocking the cabin calaboose behind him, and Rowdy stretched himself upon the floor, letting Stumpy have the cot, and dozed for a while, catching up on his sleep. Morning became afternoon, and nothing was changed. The long day dragged itself onward, and Rowdy, sated with sleeping, took to looking from the cell windows. One faced toward Bearclaw and gave him a glimpse of the straggly town. The other looked out upon a pine-clad slope with an open clearing of perhaps fifty yards between the building and the first timber. And it was while Rowdy was gazing from this second window that he suddenly stiffened with surprise, beckoning Stumpy to him.

"Do I see it?" Rowdy demanded. "Or am I loco?"

For, emerging from the timber and striding toward the window, keeping the building between himself and Bearclaw, was an eye-filling figure in black velvet garb with silver trimmings, a white shirt and a crimson sash, a bandage peeping beneath the black, flat-brimmed sombrero this caballero wore. Drawing closer to the jail-building, the apparition smiled, a white flash of teeth in the olive face. "I, senors," he announced, "am Don Sebastian Gregorio Jose de Ibarra y Alvarez. *Buenos dias.*"

"Whether it's a good day depends on your viewpoint," said the thunderstruck Rowdy.

"Last night you do the great service for me," said Don Sebastian. "To-day it is you who are in the beeg trouble. Lucky that Don Sebastian has long ears like the burro to know these things. Now the balances of justice they shall be swung, no? You would like to be free of thees *carcel,* Senor Dow?"

"You know my name?"

"Last night I see your face. In *Mejico* eet is not unknown. Once I see a reward poster with your picture. You do not look much like heem, but I, Don Sebastian, am trained in the remembering."

The caballero had drawn close enough to inspect the barred window. From his sash Don Sebastian drew a long-bladed knife with a handsome ivory handle, and this he laid between the bars. "The wood it will cheep away, no? Here is your key to freedom, senors."

He made a low, sweeping bow. "The debt eet is now paid," he said, and, turning, began striding back toward the timber.

"Just a minute," Rowdy shouted after him. "I've got a lot I want to ask you!"

But Don Sebastian Gregorio Jose de Ibarra y Alvarez did not so much as look over his shoulder; he strode onward, vanishing into the timber; and Rowdy and Stumpy stood staring at each other. But for the knife which the elegantly-dressed Mexican had left behind, they might have wondered if they'd dreamed all this.

But there was no disputing the actuality of the knife, and Don Sebastian had pointed out the purpose to which it could be put. They fell to work at once, chipping away at the wooded base in which the bars were embedded — slow, arduous work calculated to bring the sweat out on a man. Their impulse was to hurry the job; their fear was that to do so might snap the blade. They took turns, spelling each other, and they were still at the task when the early dusk of the mountain country descended. Karst came then with another tray, and, hearing his footsteps, they hastily brushed away the chips and were seated innocently upon the cot when the door opened. Karst was in a sullen mood again, making no talk and tarrying no longer than necessary. Which pleased the partners mightily. Both had bolted their food, hoping desperately that Karst wouldn't glance toward the window.

Alone, they fell to work again. When they had two of the bars freed from the wooden base, Rowdy put his strength against the iron and was able to bend these bars outward. Stumpy wormed through the opening, Rowdy shoving him from behind until Stumpy tumbled to the ground outside, smothering a litany of profanity. Rowdy had to squeeze hard to get his own broad shoulders through the window. Stumpy got a hold on him and pulled, and Rowdy found himself in a heap.

"Free, dang it!" Stumpy breathed triumphantly.

Clambering to his feet, Rowdy brushed himself off. "The first thing we'll want is our guns," he said. "Then our horses. I reckon those guns might still be in the hotel room. Come along, Stumpy."

They approached Bearclaw carefully, thankful for the twilight's mantle. They got to the cover of an alley as quickly as possible and followed the alley to the rear of the hotel. They found the window through which their visitor had entered that morning, but the sash refused to yield. "Must have locked it myself, after I let Buck Trimble out," Rowdy groaned. "Too risky breaking it." He pressed his nose against the glass and peered inside, hoping to see if the guns were on the floor; but it was now too dark.

"We've got to risk the lobby," Rowdy decided and moved resolutely towards the front of the building.

The lobby was deserted save for the thin, watery-eyed youth when they entered, and this young man's eyes snapped wide in utter astonishment. Donning a scowl black enough to scare the devil into reforming, Rowdy said, "Watch him, Stumpy. If he raises a squawk, strangle him with your bare hands and bury his carcass under an old rotten log somewhere. I'll be right back."

Hurrying down the hall, he entered the room they'd rented that morning, and, snatching their slickers from where they still lay upon the bed, probed into a corner for the discarded guns. The weapons in his hands, he came charging back to the lobby where Stumpy stood fiercely glaring at the clerk. Rowdy thrust Stumpy's slicker and gun at his partner and said, "Let's get out of here."

"Just a minute, Mr. Dow," the clerk said in a quavering voice.

The youth was probing deep under the desk, and Rowdy spun about, raising his gun, fearful that the clerk was going for a hidden weapon. But the boy's hands had come into view again, and in them was a large white envelope. "This is for you," the clerk said.

"What is this?" Rowdy demanded suspiciously.

"Look," said the clerk, "I'm new here, come out from the East for my health. I take no sides in the trouble between Rancho Del Diablo and the Shootin' Soreheads. It's no concern of mine. But I was paid to do a job, and I'm doing it. I know you're Rowdy Dow. Your name's on the register. A couple of weeks ago I was walking along Bearclaw Creek on my day off, and Captain Buck Trimble came out of the woods and spoke to me. He said you'd be showing up in Bearclaw about the twenty-first, and he gave me a hundred dollar bill and asked me to put this envelope in your hands."

Still suspicious, Rowdy took the proffered envelope and ran his thumb under the flap. Inside he found a sheaf of one hundred dollar bills which he quickly leafed through. A thousand dollars. The note that was enclosed was brief and was written in a broad, sprawling fist. It read:

Dear Dow:

Perhaps I'll be able to meet you in Bearclaw as originally planned. Perhaps not. I've reason to fear that my life is in danger, so I'm taking this chance on leaving word for you. Don't know whether I can trust the bearer of this, so I'll say no more than is necessary.

If I manage to see you, I'll be able to explain man to man the assignment I have in mind for you. If not, you'll find an explanatory document hidden in a book in my library at Rancho Del Diablo. Look for the third book from the left on the fourth shelf from the floor nearest the big door.

The enclosed sum is a retaining fee to show my sincerity.

Captain Buck Trimble.

Stumpy had been glancing nervously toward the door. "Let's get out of here," he wailed. "Let's get hold of our horses and shake the dust of this Bearclaw country."

Rowdy wordlessly handed him the note, then faced the clerk again, laying a gold piece on the desk before the youth. "You did your job, and here's extra pay. Keep your mouth shut about this and you'll get into no trouble with Karst's crew, because we'll keep shut likewise. Now tell me: what did Buck Trimble look like?"

"Well," said the youth, "he was wearing a queer sombrero, Mexican style but covered with feathers and —"

"I know! I know!" Rowdy said impatiently. "His face —"

"He was a big man, red-faced, and had a white moustache and a beak of a nose, and a regular mane of white hair. He —"

"That's enough!" said Rowdy, and, nudging Stumpy's elbow, headed his partner toward the door. Outside, they hurried around the building, seeking the shadows of the alley again.

"We're riding out, ain't we?" Stumpy demanded.

"Not to-night," Rowdy replied. "Don't you savvy, Stumpy? That wasn't Buck Trimble who came to us this morning with that Mexico City proposition. It was some impostor wearing Trimble's feathered sombrero. Just what his game was I don't know. But we've got a thousand dollars in our jeans, and we're working for Buck Trimble now — the real Buck Trimble. On top of that, there's Felicia to think about, too. We've got to get inside Rancho Del Diablo, old hoss. We've got to find out what it is that Buck Trimble wants us to do."

CHAPTER IV

A LIGHT IN THE NIGHT

They hurried along the alley toward the livery stable, a pair of men who'd suddenly found themselves gainfully employed, and Rowdy's mind was awhirl as he tried to fit the latest developments into a coherent pattern. So Captain Trimble had been impersonated that morning — impersonated by the nameless man who'd left a coat button in Rowdy's hand in the darkness of Halfway House! But the real Trimble had managed to get word to Rowdy nevertheless, and Trimble had sent along a thousand dollars to show his sincerity. That, Rowdy conceded, was sincerity with a capital S! Yet, according to Abel Karst and his Shootin' Soreheads, Buck Trimble was the devil incarnate, and Rowdy was therefore buying a pig in a poke by blindly accepting the thousand. Rowdy didn't try to fool himself. A consuming curiosity plus a memory of Felicia's frenzied face pressed against a window of Halfway House were the real factors which were drawing him to Rancho Del Diablo.

But first the partners must have their

horses, and the getting of them involved a certain risk. The young clerk at the hotel had been neutral as regarded Bearclaw affairs. The livery stable hostler might have a biased view. After all, this town belonged to Karst's crew.

Rowdy evolved no strategy as he strode rapidly along, the complaining Stumpy wheezing beside him. They would handle the hostler as the situation demanded. When they reached the rear door of the livery stable and squeezed inside that fragrant establishment, Rowdy was elated to discover that the hostler was not the grumbling man who'd admitted them early that morning. The present custodian was older than the Rockies and just about as bald on top, a guarded fellow, snaggle-toothed and whiskered. To him Rowdy said, "Those are our cayuses yonder. Saddle 'em up, will you, Pop?"

"Sure," said the oldster and fell clumsily to the task. Peering at the partners in the light of a smoky lantern a few minutes later, he said, "Ain't I seen you some-place before?"

Rowdy tensed, mindful of the ravaged bars of the cabin calaboose, mindful that the empty prison might be discovered any moment and an alarm set up. But he shrugged. "Could be, Pop. You ever been around Delmonico's restaurant in New York? Me and my partner, Mr. Jones here, used to be head waiters in that shebang."

"Do tell!" said the ancient, fumbling to tighten a cinch. "No, 'tweren't there. S-a-a-y! I seed a couple fellers dragged off to jail this morning. Couple fellers just about the build and complexion of you two jiggers!"

Rowdy had been itching to lend a hand with the saddling, to hurry it along, but he'd refrained for fear that any show of unseemly haste might further arouse the hostler's suspicion. Now Rowdy's cherubic face took on a look of horrified amazement. "Jail!" he ejaculated. "Pop, that's downright insulting! What would our old mothers say if they thought we were being mistaken for jiggers who got hauled off to jail?"

"Just the same, you look like 'em," the oldster insisted. "Danged if you don't." He slapped a saddle on Stumpy's horse and reached under the belly for the cinch. "S-a-a-y! If you busted out of Abel Karst's jail — !"

Rowdy had begun a cautious edging toward the front of the building. Now he reached and pushed at the door, shoving it wide open. Stumpy, alarm showing on his leathery face, forced a hollow guffaw.

"Shucks, Pop, we never busted out of no jail," Stumpy said soothingly. "How could we? Them bars was set as solid as a boulder in a river bed and —"

Only then did Stumpy realise his own mistake, for the hostler's bleary eyes had widened with the certainty of conviction. Truly, the fat was in the fire. But the horses were saddled and the reins in place, and Rowdy, heading back to his mount, leap-frogged into the saddle and sent a coin spinning to the hostler. That worthy automatically caught the money, and Stumpy clambered aboard his saddle, and the two, bending low, backed their mounts from the stalls and headed for the open front door.

"Stop!" the hostler squawked and went diving toward a litter of blankets in an empty stall. Probing into them, he produced an ancient pistol of tremendous size; but the partners were through the doorway as the pistol began blasting. Rowdy cursed under his breath, knowing the alarm would fetch the town running, and as his mount plunged into the street, he heard a wild outcry at the far edge of town, in the vicinity of the cabin calaboose.

"Somebody else has discovered that we busted out!" Stumpy judged. "Come on,

Rowdy! We gotta make dust!"

Bearclaw was beginning to stir to its night life, the many saloons showing light and more men moving along the planking than had been in evidence at any time since the two had first viewed this street. Now men were beginning to converge from everywhere, and someone close at hand — one of Karst's crew, obviously — set up a shout at sight of the two. A gun banged, and Rowdy's sombrero brim twitched. But Rowdy and Stumpy were now careering along the street, and they were to the edge of town before any pursuers could get into saddles. Pursuit was coming, though. Behind them they'd left a kicked-over hornets' nest, and Rowdy was quick to press the slight advantage they'd gained.

He led the way along the first trail he saw, and it wasn't until they'd galloped for half a mile, looking behind more often than they looked ahead, that either realised this was the trail that had fetched them into Bearclaw this morning. Rowdy sighed. He would have preferred the road to Rancho Del Diablo. As long as they were being chased, it would have been better to be chased toward their chosen destination; but he had only a vague idea of the location of Trimble's ranch. He'd hoped to get more exacting directions from the hostler by some subterfuge, but Stumpy's ill-chosen words had made that impossible.

When they paused for a moment to listen, they heard drumming hoofs behind them, and there was nothing to do but hasten. At least this trail was leading them into the timbered hills, and darkness might soon be their ally, though the sky was not overcast to-night; a few stars were already showing, and the moon made a yellow smudge atop the eastern hills. They rode as recklessly as they dared, bending low to avoid branches, each of them grim with the knowledge that Karst's crew knew this country far better than they did. A net might easily be spread to enmesh them.

And Karst's crew was slowly overtaking them. Of this Rowdy was sure a few miles later as they paused again to listen to the hoofbeats. But because the Shootin' Soreheads were obviously moving too fast to be cutting any sign, Rowdy hauled his horse off into the screening underbrush, Stumpy following suit, and the two stood with hands clasped firmly over their mounts' nostrils, stood thus for many minutes until a dark, rushing river of riders swept past them and on up the trail.

"Look at 'em go!" Stumpy whispered

hoarsely. "Now ain't that just like some jiggers — stampedin' through life like they had to cram the next five years into to-night!"

"They'll be back," Rowdy observed. "Sooner or later they'll realise we're not ahead of them, and then they'll start looking for tracks."

He began leading his horse through a maze of lodgepole pine, Stumpy trailing after him, and it was darker than the inside of a boot back here in the timber, and the underfooting was slippery with fallen needles. Shortly they came upon a game trail and, mounting, they followed this trail northward.

"As good a direction as any," Rowdy opined. "When Karst finds we've shook him, he'll suppose we headed back towards Bearclaw. Likely he'll then lope along the road to Rancho Del Diablo. He'll be convinced now that we're lined up with Buck Trimble."

And so they moved onward through the night; the moon rose and a little of its light managed to seep down through the tangle of tree tops. The miles fell behind them, and they would have been hopelessly lost except that they managed to catch an occasional glimpse of the stars. The trail twisted and turned, as erratic as a colt the first time out of a corral, but eventually it converged with another broader trail, and the partners, following this, soon became aware that they had manœuvred back to the main trail.

"The question," said Rowdy, "is whether Karst is above or below us."

They paused, listening intently, but they only heard the normal sounds of the night. An owl glided overhead, hunting; a rodent squeaked somewhere off in the woods; a creek bickered in the far distance. Moving onward, they took a turn of the trail, and Stumpy, pointing ahead in surprise, said, "Danged if that ain't Halfway House!"

Rowdy's fingers clamped hard on Stumpy's arm. "Easy!" Rowdy said. "There's a light burning in the downstairs floor."

They were on the edge of a clearing with the huge, two-storied log building looming ahead, looking more ghostly in the pale moonlight than it had in the storm-ravaged darkness of the previous night. Had Karst's crew stopped here? There was no horse in the yard, no smoke rising from the chimney, no other sign of occupancy save that light. The partners walked their horses cautiously forward, but a bit chain jingled and saddle leather creaked, and instantly the light was extinguished, the windows to the front of the building showing black.

"Now what do you make of that?" Rowdy said.

Dismounting, he climbed quickly and silently to the gallery, eased his gun from its holster, and, gun in hand, suddenly stepped through the window he'd broken last night. Into the darkened bar-room, he moved away from the window, putting his back to the wall and standing silently. Nothing stirred. Plucking a cartridge from his belt, Rowdy tossed it along the floor. The shell made a rattling, echoing noise, but after that the silence clamped down hard again.

"Stumpy!" Rowdy called cautiously. "Come on in. He must have headed out the back door."

Stumpy was silhouetted briefly in the window opening; the darkness swallowed him and he was at Rowdy's side.

"Help me find a lamp," Rowdy said. "I'm going to risk a light. I want to have a look around. You suppose that whoever was here was one of our friends of last night?"

They groped their way across the barroom, Stumpy cursing as he collided with one of the several gaming tables. Rowdy was about to venture a match when Stumpy said, "Here's the lamp. And the chimney's still hot!" A match scraped, blossomed into light, Stumpy touched fire to the lamp's wick, and Rowdy, the hammer of his gun eared back, spun quickly, sweeping the entire room with his glance. There was the bar, with the dead proprietor where they'd laid him, but now a blanket, probably fetched from one of the upstairs rooms, had been spread over the body. And upon the table where Stumpy had found a lamp were dishes and a partly-eaten meal.

"Jumpin' Jehosaphat!" Stumpy quavered. "It ain't possible that dead jigger was having hisself something to eat!"

Rowdy crossed the bar-room and ventured up the stairs, and no one challenged him. One by one he looked into the rooms, giving special attention to the one where Don Sebastian had lain the night before and to the room where he'd seen Felicia's face pressed against the window. The wind, sweeping around the sash, had obliterated her message in the dust of the sill. The hall littered with many matches from Rowdy's seeking, he returned to the ground floor where Stumpy kept a wary vigil.

"Nobody here," Rowdy announced.

"Let's get moving," Stumpy said. "We don't know whether Karst might come lopin' along."

Rowdy strode over and lifted the blanket

from the face of the dead proprietor. "The only decent thing to do is bury the gent," he said. "I figured to leave that chore to the law of Bearclaw, but the only law is Karst's, and we're not liable to be on speaking terms. See if you can rustle up a shovel, Stumpy."

"Maybe we'd better leave him lie, Rowdy. We don't want that killin' pinned on us."

"Makes no never mind. The way we stack up in Karst's tally book now, we're probably getting the blame for everything but the War of 1812. This gent needs planting. Rustle a shovel, Stumpy."

Stumpy, obviously not enthusiastic, began prowling the bar-room and finally took a look behind the bar. His shout fetched Rowdy, who found his partner pointing to a trap-door set in the floor. Rowdy grasped the ring and raised this door and saw the dark maw of a cellar below. He lighted a match and tossed it downwards; the match quickly winked out. His gun in his hand again, Rowdy cautiously began descending the cellar steps. "Fetch a lamp, Stumpy," he said.

Stumpy followed after him, lamp in hand. This cellar was small, stone-walled and dirt-floored and almost filled with cases and barrels, most of them apparently containing liquors. One case, an open box, aroused Stumpy's interest, and he delved into it.

"Skyrockets!" he announced in astonishment. "And Roman candles and firecrackers! Now what do you make of this, Rowdy? It's a long time till the Fourth o' July!"

"Must be some fireworks left over from a celebration last year," Rowdy judged. "Look, there's some tools."

A shovel and a crowbar stood in one littered corner; near these implements a saw, a hammer, and a box of nails perched atop a packing case. Rowdy took the shovel, and they climbed out of the cellar and closed the trap-door. The lamp placed upon the bar, Rowdy took a look around the room again. "That back door!" he ejaculated. "It's closed and barred from the inside! Whoever was here *couldn't* have left that way. Or did you bar the door while I was upstairs?"

"Never touched it," Stumpy said.

Rowdy frowned. "A man had a lamp burning here when we rode up. That man was having something to eat. He doused the light and lit out when he heard us. But how? He isn't in the building, that's sure. And he couldn't have come out the front way, because we'd have seen him."

Stumpy said, "I don't like this place. I don't like it at all!"

"Neither do I," Rowdy agreed. "Let's get the chore done."

They extinguished the lamp and climbed through the window, fetching the shovel along, and their first move was to place their horses in the stable so the mounts wouldn't be seen if Karst's crew came along. In the soft loam near the stable they began digging a grave. Taking turns at the shovel, they made the dirt fly, pausing from time to time to rest themselves and listen for any alien sound. Soon they had the grave deep enough, and they returned to the bar-room, and between them managed to carry the dead proprietor outside. Leaving the body wrapped in the blanket, they lowered it into the grave.

"Seems like we shouldn't just throw dirt in his face and call it a day," Rowdy said. "A few words should be spoken. Or a song sung. You know any funeral oration, Stumpy?"

Stumpy wrinkled his face in thought, and then inspiration came. "I know a poem," he said helpfully.

"Well, reel it off then."

Their sombreros in their hands, they took a stand near the edge of the grave, and Stumpy began solemnly reciting:

"Now Lizzy was a lady, although her
past was shady,

And her morals weren't exactly what a gent would call refined.
She had made an honest livin' at gettin' and at givin'
And her heart was awful big, and her heart was awful kind.
One night she was a-sittin' at her window with her knittin'
When a bow-legg'd gent came lurching up the boardwalk full of beer.
He was feelin' mighty restive, and his mood was sort of festive, and —"

"Just a minute!" Rowdy managed to interject. "Somehow it doesn't sound exactly appropriate for the occasion. We'll say him a silent prayer and then get to work with the shovel."

Shortly the dirt was flying again, and thus this nameless man they had known so very briefly was properly buried. Rowdy marked the spot with the largest stone he could find in a brief search, then headed back to Halfway House. They climbed through the window and leaned the shovel against the wall, and Stumpy said, "That's that. We'd best be moving along. But I'm thinking that the jigger we just planted would shorely feel we had a drink on the house comin' to us."

"Shhhh!" Rowdy admonished him, his

fingers again clamping on Stumpy's arm. "Did you hear it?"

Out yonder, to the front of the building, saddle leather had creaked, and voices reached them through the broken window. Rowdy crept toward the window and peered cautiously outside, Stumpy at his elbow. And there in the clearing, darkness against darkness, were the shapes of waiting men.

CHAPTER V

THE PADLOCKED GATE

Abel Karst had caught up with them. They could hear his gruff voice, and Rowdy thought he could make out the solid form of the man, and it took no mathematical wizard to put together the two and two that accounted for Karst's presence here. Karst and the other dispossessed ranchers had plunged headlong up the trail in pursuit of Rowdy Dow and Stumpy Grampis, and, galloping to a point beyond Halfway House, had come to the realisation that their quarry had somehow eluded them. Now they had turned back, and, whether they were aware of it or not, penned the fugitives in the mountain tavern.

"We could slip out the back door," Stumpy whispered hoarsely.

"Wouldn't work," Rowdy decided. "We'd have to get to the barn and fork our cayuses, and somebody would see us crossing the clearing."

Their eyes growing more accustomed to the darkness, they saw that the Shootin' Soreheads were sitting their saddles in a tight knot, no one as yet making a move to dismount. Karst's crew were talking among themselves, and snatches of the talk floated to the partners. The question seemed to be whether it would be worth while to search Halfway House, some holding that they'd best be getting on down the trail. "Those jiggers took to the woods and are high-tailing south," someone said distinctly. "Every minute we waste is putting 'em farther away."

Stumpy eased his gun out of leather. "If they start inside, I'm scattering a few slugs," he whispered. "That should send 'em streakin' for cover. Maybe, in the confusion, we'll get a chance to run for the barn."

"Wait!" Rowdy countered, seeing the sense of Stumpy's proposed strategy and seeing also a way of improving upon the plan. "Hurry down into the cellar and get an armload of those skyrockets. We'll *really* startle those gents!"

Stumpy slid off into the darkness, hurrying as fast as he could but making very little noise. Crouched by the window, Rowdy waited what seemed an endless time. He heard the creak of the trap-door as Stumpy hoisted it, but he also heard the creak of saddle leather as Karst himself dismounted.

Karst said, "It won't take more than ten

minutes for the bunch of us to have a look in every corner of the place. I'm going to comb 'er fine."

Hurry, Stumpy, Rowdy thought. *Hurry, old horse!*

"We'd do better to head straight for Rancho Del Diablo and block the road," someone grumbled. "That's where those jiggers are floggin' their cayuses right now."

What in thunder was keeping Stumpy, Rowdy wondered dismally, and was cold with the remembrance that at least four people had already disappeared from this accursed place under mysterious circumstances. Had Stumpy, too, been swallowed up?

Karst had taken a stride toward the gallery; so far only he had dismounted. "A couple of you jiggers have a look in the barn," he ordered. "The rest of you trail along with me."

"Here yuh are, Rowdy," Stumpy whispered at his partner's elbow and pressed several skyrockets into Rowdy's hands.

There was no time to be lost. Rowdy quickly propped four of the skyrockets against the window-sill, hoping that he was setting them at the proper angle to make them go where he wanted them to go. Stretching on his stomach on the floor,

Stumpy beside him, he fumbled for matches. Both men got fire aglow and touched it to fuses, and, sputtering, the sky-rockets went sailing through the broken window. The tilt had been just right! The rockets cleared the gallery railing and arched straight towards the huddled horsemen, sparks trailing. Themselves momentarily blinded by this pyrotechnic display, Rowdy and Stumpy nevertheless moved hastily. Leaping through the window, they ran along the gallery, vaulted the railing and headed for the barn at a hard run.

No one challenged them. Off yonder the Shootin' Soreheads were fighting plunging horses, consternation reigning among Karst's crew. Karst's own horse had reared and was bolting, with Karst frantically trying to get a hold of the reins again. This Rowdy saw in one quick backward glance as he gained the stable door. Then the partners were inside the barn and out again, dragging their mounts behind them. Vaulting into saddles, they hit for the closest timber.

Bullets sped them on their way. Some of the Shootin' Soreheads had seen them, of course, but Karst's crew was far too busy to make a concerted effort to block the escape. Not in these first frantic minutes. Men were cursing angrily and getting in each other's way, horses crashing against horses in a mad mêlée. But Rowdy had expected to gain no more than a slight advantage with his ruse, and as the timber swallowed the partners, he heard the shouts of men as the pursuit fanned out to take the trail.

Whereupon Rowdy turned due west, Stumpy blindly following him, cut across the main-trail and plunged into the timber on the far side of it. Almost at once they were ascending, for the ground tilted abruptly upward, and very soon they had to dismount and lead their horses. Underbrush was thick, and deadfall logs were strewn everywhere, and they could hear men calling one to another from all directions.

"Dang it all, Rowdy," Stumpy complained, "we ain't making no more speed than a hobbled hatrack. This is just askin' to be caught. Let's find a level trail and burn leather."

Rowdy made no reply, and shortly Stumpy wailed, "This is just like climbing straight up a wall."

They were ascending a ridge that ran north and south, a ridge so thickly timbered as to make progress almost impossible. But the shouts of the pursuers were growing dimmer, and Rowdy, noting this with silent satisfaction, toiled onward and upward. After an hour they could no longer hear Karst's men, but still Rowdy continued the ascent. A good deal of the night was gone, and very little moonlight penetrated here. Bushes scraped at the partners, and every footfall had to be tested. They lost track of time and distance and were a pair of wanderers in a nightmare, but at long last they stood on the rocky summit of the ridge.

"Whew!" Stumpy exclaimed. "It's shore nice to be out of them trees. Rowdy, I'm hoping I never see a tree again the rest of my life."

"We're heading down the other side," Rowdy said relentlessly. "Come along, Stumpy. Into the trees."

Still leading the way, Rowdy began the descent, Stumpy swearing along behind him. It was the reverse of the route they'd just followed; now they had to brake their heels against a slope, but again bushes scraped them and every footfall had to be tested, and there was underbrush to fight and deadfall logs to skirt or clamber over. Again they lost track of time and distance; the calves of their legs ached, and they slipped on the needle-strewn underfooting more than once. But it was the horses that really concerned Rowdy; they had to be got down this slope with no broken legs.

Just as the first dawn light streaked the east, they came to level ground and found the timber not as thick as it had been, and shortly they reached the broadest trail they'd yet come across in this Bearclaw country — a trail that might have called itself a road without being too careless with the truth.

"Now this is some better," Rowdy said, climbing aboard his horse. Stumpy also mounted, and they began following the broad trail to the north. In the first grey light, Stumpy gazed back up the slope and sleeved sweat from his forehead. "Dang it all, Rowdy," Stumpy said sternly, "I'm getting too old for the sort of fool nonsense a feller runs into when he's taggin' around with you!"

The trail began paralleling a brawling, willow-fringed creek that came down out of the north. Rowdy, studying the creek speculatively, said, "Stumpy, if I've got this country figured out right, this is Bearclaw Creek. It heads on south to Bearclaw town. Rancho Del Diablo must be somewhere to the north-west of here. Of course it could be below us. But the town is south — that's for certain. I think we'll keep on going in this direction."

Both were tired and both were hungry, but at least they were sitting in saddles again, and their good humour restored itself; even Stumpy began to grin as they rode along. "I've got to hand it to you at that, Rowdy," he said grudgingly. "You shore shook Karst's crew off our trail."

"Nothing to it," Rowdy said with an airy wave of his hand. "Just using the old think-box, partner. After all, I did plenty of dodging when I was riding the owl-hoot, and we've done our share of it since. A fellow learns as he goes along."

"Me, I'd have looked for a stretch where I could 'a' sunk the hooks into my hoss," Stumpy said. "Seemed loco when you took the slow way."

"When a fellow's getting chased, his instinct is to make speed," Rowdy said pedantically. "And that's just what the galoots who are chasing him expect him to do. Karst and his boys know this country. As soon as they got control of their horses after the skyrocket stampede, I'll bet they fanned out pronto to cover all the trails. So I fooled them by avoiding the trails. The ridge was slow going, but that's exactly why they didn't think to hunt for us on the ridge."

"You really outsmarted 'em," Stumpy vowed, a vast admiration in his voice.

"Nothing to it," Rowdy repeated. "Right now we've got yon ridge between us and them, and they're over the hump somewhere, chasing their tails around in circles."

Stumpy guffawed loudly. "Wait till the pore jackasses finally wake up to the fact that we're plumb out of the vicinity. They'll know they're up against a couple of smart jaspers when they try cuttin' sign on Rowdy Dow and Stumpy Grampis." He swatted angrily at his left ear. "Dang that fly!"

"That's no fly!" Rowdy shouted, for, far behind them, a rifle's report split the morning's silence, the hills catching the sound and sending the echoes chasing each other. This broad trail had been running straight as an arrow for nearly a mile, and, looking backward, Rowdy saw the group of riders who were coming in hot pursuit. "Karst's crew!" Rowdy ejaculated. "Hump it, Stumpy!"

Bending low over their saddle-horns, they used spurs, lifting the horses to a high gallop and thundering along the trail. Rifle bullets peppered about them, and the partners, armed only with six-shooters, kept their guns cased, knowing they were outranged. Ahead was a turn of the trail; once around it they were out of the danger from flying lead. But still they quirted and spurred; their only hope was to hold their lead and try to lengthen it. The trail ran on, sometimes straight, sometimes taking an abrupt turn, and thus they had intermittent glimpses of the pursuing riders. Karst's crew was concentrating on closing the distance, and they only fired sporadically. But those singing bullets were enough to keep the partners' minds on their work.

"Hope they didn't change horses somewhere along the way!" Rowdy shouted. "Otherwise their mounts should be as tired as ours."

And then, suddenly, Rowdy was hauling on the reins, his horse rearing, for dead ahead the trail was blocked. The creek that paralleled the trail had taken an abrupt swing to the east, crossing the trail, and spanning the creek at this point was a small rustic bridge. Just beyond the bridge a fence loomed, a high, six-strand barbed wire fence with a huge padlocked gate. And because this was most obviously the entrance to Rancho Del Diablo, Rowdy saw with startling clarity how Abel Karst had come to be so close behind them.

Karst had suspected from the first that they would be heading for Buck Trimble's ranch. Some of Karst's crew had even been in favour of giving up any careful search for the fugitives and hurrying instead to the road to Rancho Del Diablo to block it. The

Shootin' Soreheads, then, had followed the mountain trail southward on the far side of the ridge, skirted the ridge and cut across to this broad trail which was the road to Trimble's ranch. And Karst, patrolling the road, had stumbled upon the partners. By climbing the ridge and descending to the other side — good enough strategy as far as it went — Rowdy and Stumpy had unwittingly made the well-known hop from the frying-pan to the fire. And worse, with Karst's crew again hard behind them, the padlocked gate ahead made a dead end.

But it was not the formidable barrier that was holding Rowdy's eye. Beyond the gate at least twenty riders sat their saddles, drawn here doubtless by the sounds of gunfire and pursuit, and from a distance these riders appeared to be Mexican vaqueros. They wore the cone-shaped straw sombreros and the cotton trousers of riders from manana land, but their faces, dusky, expressionless as so many stone idols, were heavy-beaked and savage. Seeing them, Rowdy remembered that the man with the feathered sombrero who'd visited him in Bearclaw had maintained that the crew of Rancho Del Diablo were descendants of the ancient Aztecs. Rowdy could believe it now.

One among them had dismounted and

was apparently probing at the padlock with a key, and when the gate swung open and this one stepped through, Rowdy saw that he was a white man. And apparently the leader of these savage riders, for he swung his arm in signal, stepping up into his saddle as he did so, and the whole group came swarming through the gate. Glancing behind, Rowdy saw that the Shootin' Soreheads had burst around a turn and were roaring down the road, but Karst's crew, suddenly aware of the riders pouring from Rancho Del Diablo, slithered their horses to a stop, and the guns began banging.

On both sides. Karst's outfit was throwing lead and so were the vaqueros, these two groups of long-time enemies suddenly staging a war, with Rowdy and Stumpy caught in the middle of it. Rowdy, bellowing an order to his partner, slipped from his horse and let the mount bolt and flattened himself to the ground beside the trail, Stumpy lighting to crowd close to him. The Aztec riders came thundering across the bridge and charged past, a half-dozen of them flinging themselves from their saddles to swarm over Rowdy and Stumpy, pinning them to the ground.

Struggling, Rowdy had a glimpse down the trail. Karst's crew, greatly outnumbered, had weighed discretion against valour and was doing the sensible thing. Turning tail, they went streaking southward, their guns still banging. The vaqueros didn't pursue them far. They soon turned back to where their fellows had dragged Rowdy and Stumpy to a stand; and the white man among them pressed his horse forward and sat his saddle looking down at the prisoners.

"What fetched you here?" he demanded.

He was a little fellow, dressed in conventional range garb with two six-shooters belted around his thin middle, and he couldn't possibly have weighed over one hundred and twenty pounds if he were wringing wet and had his pockets full of rocks. His face was thin and ferret-like, his eyes close-set and small and cold, and he had two large protruding teeth that worried his lower lip. All in all he looked more like a gopher than anything possibly could that was equipped with only two feet, and Rowdy, gazing at him, remembered Abel Karst's reference to the segundo who ramrodded Buck Trimble's crew. This, then, was the kill-crazy Gopher Kid.

"I'm Rowdy Dow," Rowdy announced. "And this is my partner, Stumpy Grampis. Likely your boss, Buck Trimble, has spoken to you about us. We're mighty obliged for your taking Karst's bunch off our necks."

He hardly knew what reception his statements would receive, but he wasn't prepared for the hysterical giggle that came from the Gopher Kid. The Kid was suddenly a man mighty pleased with himself, but there was nothing comforting about his delight. Not for Rowdy Dow.

"This is luck," the Kid said, but he was addressing his crew. "Tie their hands behind them and fetch them along. Toward that old cottonwood up the creek. It will be as good a place as any to hang the pair of them."

CHAPTER VI

"QUETZALCOATL!"

For the past twenty-four hours, most of which had been spent in the cabin calaboose at Bearclaw or in a futile effort to elude the Shootin' Soreheads, Rowdy had leaned toward the opinion that the world would have been a sunnier place if Abel Karst had forgotten to be born. Now Rowdy was suddenly deciding that this same Abel Karst was a prince among men and worth his weight in solid platinum. Gazing longingly to the south, Rowdy hoped to glimpse Karst returning to carry a war back to the riders of Rancho Del Diablo. Far better to be in the hands of Karst than prisoners of this sadistic Gopher Kid who was making talk of a necktie party. But Karst was far gone; even the dust of his departure had settled. Scant hope for help from that quarter.

Whereupon Rowdy fixed a cold stare upon the Gopher Kid. "Now see here — !" Rowdy began to bluster, but it had a hollow ring even to his own ears. Vaqueros had a tight hold on both partners, and Rowdy's hands were being lashed behind him while

Stumpy was likewise tied. Verbal intimidation would be so much wasted breath. Two of the vaqueros came leading the bolted horses of the partners, and they were boosted to their own saddles. Their guns were still in their holsters, but those weapons seemed as far away as Chicago on a foggy day.

Pocketed by the riders with the Gopher Kid riding up front, the group left the trail and began skirting the creek and the high fence to the north-east, the timbered ridge rearing above them to their right. The Kid, delighted beyond measure by the prospect he had in mind, giggled from time to time; his stony-faced followers talked low-voiced. A sprinkling of border Spanish salted their tongue, but the language of manana-land was sadly corrupted in their mouths. At least it wasn't the language Rowdy had heard along the brimstone border. These riding riddles had a dialect of their own.

All of which might have been extremely entrancing under other circumstances, but Rowdy could take no pleasure in making a linguistic discovery in what might well be his last moments. Not by a jugful! He stole a glance at Stumpy and saw that his partner was both glum and angry. He had ridden a lot of miles with Stumpy, and a great anger began growing in Rowdy, an anger that their trail should come to such an end. But still he kept silent. Words would not prevail against the Gopher Kid, he judged.

Less than a mile from the padlocked gate, the group turned and began climbing the ridge, which was not so steep here. A hundred yards up the slope, on a shelf of level ground, stood an ancient cottonwood, its lowest branches a dozen feet in the air. Beneath this tree the riders halted. At a nod from the buck-toothed Kid, two of the vaqueros shook out lariats and sent them sailing over a limb; the nooses were dropped over the heads of the partners, and the ropes were drawn taut and fastened to the bole of the tree.

All it would take now to leave Rowdy and Stumpy dangling would be for someone to swat their horses; but this was apparently not the Kid's plan. The Kid, his cold little eyes dancing with delight, was seemingly of a mind to make a regular fiesta of the affair. The bridles were yanked from the horses of the partners, and then the group moved a short distance down the slope and sat their saddles, watching.

Rowdy was beginning to sweat. Sooner or later his horse and Stumpy's would fall to cropping, and then the mounts would move out from beneath them, leaving them strangling and kicking. This might happen in a minute or in an hour, and the Gopher Kid was obviously prepared to wait. Trimble's segundo sat his saddle grinning, his Indian followers watching expressionless, their eyes glittering. Stumpy began cursing them all roundly.

Rowdy echoed his partner's sentiments in his heart. Just why the Gopher Kid had decided to dispose of them upon learning of their identity, he didn't know. And he hadn't intended to ask. If a man had to die, he could at least die with dignity and in silence; to begin talking might mean to begin begging, and Rowdy was sure that no appeal would reach very deep into the Kid. Here was a man who delighted in witnessing death, a man truly kill-crazy. Yet there was no weapon left to Rowdy but his tongue, and he said, "Captain Trimble's going to be mighty angry about this when he hears the news, Kid!"

The Gopher Kid had dragged a Durham sack from his pocket. His fingers busy at shaping a cigarette, he looked at Rowdy over his work.

"So — ?" said the Kid.

"Sure," said Rowdy. "Maybe this is just a hospitable custom of Rancho Del Diablo, to hang anybody who comes snooping near the fence, but it happens we were invited. Trimble figured to put us on the payroll."

"Then I'm saving Trimble money," said the Kid with that hysterical giggle of his. "You won't cost him anything dead!"

The letter Trimble had left with the Bear-claw desk-clerk was still in Rowdy's possession. He'd shoved it down into his boot-top, his favourite repository for valuables; and the only search these vaqueros had made had been to run their hands lightly over both partners in search of hideout guns at the time of their capture. Rowdy now wondered desperately whether the letter would make any impression on the Kid and sensed, somehow, that it wouldn't. His horse lowered its head and tugged at a tuft of grass. Rowdy pressed his knees hard against the horse and said, "Whoa! Whoa!" frantically.

The Gopher Kid watched this with an intense eagerness and was shaken by macabre mirth. The Gopher Kid was truly having a time for himself. "So you're going to work for Captain Trimble," he said. "Well, it won't be long. It won't be long." This convulsed him again, and his laughter was a high-pitched squeak in the morning's silence.

Rowdy's sweat was blinding him, and he

cast an agonised glance at Stumpy and saw that Stumpy's horse, too, had started cropping. Stumpy had quit his litany of profanity, thus giving Rowdy a chance to talk, but now Stumpy said, "To hell with 'em, Rowdy, old hoss. They got their necks bowed to see us dancing. Don't waste your breath on 'em."

And then, suddenly, one of the Indian riders below was stirred from his immobility. "Quetzalcoatl!" he shrieked. *"Quetzalcoatl!"* An arm raised, he pointed a quivering brown finger up the slope to a point that must have been above the cottonwood and to the left of it, for Rowdy, craning his neck, could see nothing. But every Aztec's face was lifted in that direction, and every face registered awe and horror, and at once all these vaqueros were imbued with a frantic desire to get out of the vicinity — and fast. They spun their horses and went clattering down the slope, and Rowdy's horse — to his horror — showed a desire to follow them. The mount took a step forward and Rowdy cried, "Easy, boy! Easy!"

The Gopher Kid, his face twitching and a great wrath riding him, was shouting after his fleeing crew. "Come back, damn you!" he cried, but they were deaf to him. The Kid spent a moment heaping obscenity upon the departing riders, and then spurred after them. Halfway to the bottom of the slope, the Kid reined short, swivelled in his saddle, dragged a six-shooter from his right-hand holster and emptied it in the direction the rider had pointed who had started the wild exodus. Then the Kid was galloping again, trailing after his crew, and all of them were quickly lost from Rowdy's sight.

A minute went by and another — many minutes — and the Rancho Del Diablo riders did not return. Remembering the wild fear that had lashed them, Rowdy judged that nothing short of dynamite would budge them back in this direction. And whoever or whatever had spurred them to flight put in no appearance. Silence clamped down and peace reigned upon the hills; but the situation of Rowdy and Stumpy had in no way been improved. The nooses were still around their necks, and they were still doomed to die when their horses walked out from under them.

"Now what do you make of it, Rowdy?" Stumpy demanded wonderingly, his predicament forgotten for the moment. "Who is this Quetzalcoatl jigger who scared the liver out of them Injuns?"

"I've heard the name," Rowdy said. "That fellow who came to Bearclaw wearing the feathered sombrero mentioned him. I remember now! He was claiming his crew were descendants of the Aztecs. You recollect, Stumpy? He said that some of them had claimed they'd seen this Quetzalcoatl here in Montana. Quetzalcoatl was one of the Aztec gods."

"No wonder they stampeded," Stumpy said. "But I wish this god would fly down here on his golden wings and take these damned ropes off our necks!"

"Maybe we haven't lived right," Rowdy said. "Me, I think that Indian was smoking the wrong stuff and fancied he saw what he saw. All he had to do was shout that name and the rest of them were ready to start running."

"But the Kid wasn't scared out," Stumpy argued. "And the Kid shot at *something* up yonder on the slope."

"The Kid," said Rowdy, "is crazier than a bobtailed horse in fly time." He shrugged. "Maybe there *was* somebody up on the slope — maybe there wasn't. He isn't helping us, anyway. Wonder if I could get my fingers on the knots holding your wrists?"

They were almost stirrup to stirrup, and Rowdy tried leaning toward his partner, but there wasn't enough slack in the rope around his neck to allow for manœuvring.

Stumpy made the same effort, but their fingers didn't meet. Sweating again, Rowdy lifted a foot from one stirrup and eased himself sideways in his saddle so that his back was to Stumpy. Stumpy did likewise, and they managed to touch fingers. But Rowdy's horse took a forward step, and Rowdy had to drop his leg to the stirrup again and press his knees hard, imploring the horse to behave itself, promising it all the oats a horse could eat in two lifetimes.

"Let's try 'er again," Stumpy suggested when Rowdy had got his horse to standing.

"Listen!" Rowdy cried. "Hoofbeats! Someone's coming below."

"That confounded Gopher Kid!" Stumpy judged.

Rowdy was of the same opinion. Only one rider was approaching, and it was therefore most likely Trimble's segundo. The Kid had none of his crew's superstitious dread of whatever had showed itself on the hillside, and the Kid would be coming back to make sure the chore at the cottonwood was finished properly. But to the utter astonishment of the partners, the rider who hove into view got a glimpse of them and came riding up the hill, was the elegantly-clad Mexican they had first met on a stormy trail and who had later made possible their escape from Karst's calaboose in Bearclaw.

No mistaking that black velvet garb with the silver trimmings, nor the white flash of teeth in an olive face that was Don Sebastian's smile. The caballero rode a black horse, as eye-catching as himself, and sat a silver-encrusted saddle. Pulling to a halt directly below them, he swept away his flat-brimmed sombrero and made a bow.

"I, senors," he said, "am Don Sebastian Gregorio Jose de Ibarra y Alvarez."

"We've finally caught on to that," Rowdy said. "Now will you be so kind as to hop up here and lift these ropes from around our necks."

"One moment, Senor Dow," said Don Sebastian, making no move to stir himself from the saddle. "You did for me the great service when I am heet on the head." He indicated the bandage which still peeped from beneath his replaced sombrero. "But yesterday I am getting you out of the *carcel.* The score it ees evened, no?"

"Sure," said Rowdy. "This will put you one up on us. Just go get yourself hit on the head again anytime, old horse, and we'll be glad to tote you off to bed."

"Ha!" said Don Sebastian. "You make the great joke, eh, Senor Dow?"

"I'm laughing fit to kill," Rowdy declared.

"Come on, Alvarez. The Rancho Del Diablo crowd may be around here someplace. We'd sure like to make ourselves scarce before they show back."

Don Sebastian shrugged. "First I wish to strike — what you call heem? — the bargain. While the rope ees around your neck, I have got the advantage, no? I help you, senors — you help me. Eet ees a fair proposition?"

"I'm always buying pigs in pokes," Rowdy said irritably. "Well, what do we have to do to get you to keep us from hanging?"

"It is my weesh to get inside the fence which ees surrounding Rancho Del Diablo. When I try heem alone, I get shot full of holes. But with the asseestance of two such brave caballeros, who knows?" He shrugged again. "The bargain eet interests you, no?"

"Fair enough," said Rowdy. "Just between me and you and the gatepost, Don Sebastian, we hanker to get inside that fence ourselves. Lift these ropes. We'll make the try together."

"One more theeng," Don Sebastian murmured, raising his hand. "The bargain eet is not yet complete. When we get inside, you shall asseest me in getting a certain article. If you get it, you weel turn it over to me. And you shall not ask the questions, no?"

"Look," said Rowdy, "do we have to throw in a first mortgage on our front teeth, too? Very well! We'll play your game all the way. That damn' Gopher Kid is likely to be back any minute. What is this gadget we're to help you lay your hands on with no questions asked?"

"The feathered sombrero," said Don Sebastian. "The queer sombrero wheech Captain Buck Treemble wears. That, senors, is the theeng I am after."

CHAPTER VII

WAYS AND MEANS

Later, the ropes removed from the partners' necks and their hands untied by Don Sebastian, the three rode down the slope together. They were faced toward Rancho Del Diablo, but Rowdy took a long backward look and saw, far above, a jutting rock which stood out like a white scar against the darkness of timber. There, he judged, was where Quetzalcoatl had made an appearance; from such a stand who ever had frightened the Aztecs could command a broad sweep of country. A six-shooter wouldn't carry to the rock from where Rowdy now observed it — which was approximately the spot where the Gopher Kid had done his angry firing. The Kid then had let wrath dominate whatever he possessed in the way of good sense.

Stumpy, too, was looking backward, but that leathery little man was not concerned with gods at the moment; a more earthly thought was in him. "I'm hungry!" Stumpy wailed.

"Me, too," Rowdy agreed. "You don't happen to be packing any food in your saddle-bag, Don Sebastian?"

The caballero brightened. "You like frijoles, senor?"

"Frijoles," Rowdy said, "are my favourite fruit. Trot 'em out."

Don Sebastian looked sad. "*Ay de mi!* Alas, I have no frijoles. Only cold beef and beescuits."

"That sounds like man-fodder," Rowdy said. "We're not fussy. I'd even boil one of my boots if I thought there was any nourishment in it."

"Ees twice now theese food is useful to you," said Don Sebastian. "I am come to Bearclaw to get it when I find you two in the *carcel.*"

The food passed along, the partners ate and then slaked their thirst from Bearclaw Creek, the caballero sitting his saddle watchfully while the two were down on their stomachs beside the stream. Peace still held the hills and the trio might have been a million miles from the rest of humanity, but Alvarez was constantly vigilant. This Rowdy was quick to note. He had blindly cast his lot with Don Sebastian, and it behooved him to make an accurate gauge of the man. At first look the caballero had appeared to be no more than a Mexican fop, pretty to the eye but as useless as a stuffed horse. Now

Rowdy was beginning to sense that Don Sebastian might be a good man to have around in a tight corner.

"I'm mighty curious," Rowdy said when they'd mounted again, "to know what took you out of Halfway House so fast the other night. And how did you come by that horse? You didn't have one when we found you."

"The horse I had staked out," Don Sebastian explained. "I was afoot when I get the bomp on the head. Afterwards I go to where I left the horse and he ees still there. Ees good, no?"

"That doesn't explain why you rushed out of the place after we put you to bed."

Don Sebastian smiled his flashy smile, shaking an admonishing finger at Rowdy. "The question you don' ask, remember? Eet is part of the bargain."

"Just the same," Rowdy said, "I can't help being curious."

Don Sebastian shrugged. "Asking the questions, eet is good exercise for — what you call them? — the tonsils. I make the *magnifico* gesture. You ask three questions, senor. But I don't answer them."

"Say, that's mighty big of you!" Rowdy observed. "Do you know a girl named Felicia, a Mexican probably?"

Don Sebastian's eyes darkened, and he

sombrely kissed his hand and blew the kiss in the direction of Rancho Del Diablo. "I don' answer," he said.

He knows her, all right, Rowdy judged, and some pieces of a puzzle began to fall into place. Don Sebastian had likely been headed toward Halfway House the night before last. And Felicia had been at the mountain tavern. The caballero had been reconnoitring when someone had clouted him — possibly that cadaverous man who'd left his coat button in Rowdy's hand and then later appeared in Bearclaw wearing the feathered sombrero. Don Sebastian, aroused from unconsciousness that night at Halfway House, had taken out after the cadaverous man who'd dragged Felicia from the place. But Don Sebastian had been afoot, and by the time he'd gotten his horse, he'd lost the trail. The next day he'd been in Bearclaw for supplies and thus had been able to help Rowdy and Stumpy escape from Karst's calaboose. And now Don Sebastian wanted to get inside the padlocked gate, for the caballero was certain that Felicia had been taken to Rancho Del Diablo.

But: "What about that feathered sombrero?" Rowdy asked. "What makes it so valuable?"

"When I have got my hands on eet, I tell

you, maybe," said Don Sebastian. "Ees one more question for you to ask which I don' answer."

"You're the most exasperating galoot I've met in a month of Sundays," Rowdy complained. "You've got a lot of names. Is Quetzalcoatl an extra one you use sometimes?"

"Quetzalcoatl? Ees feathered serpent god of the Aztecs. What makes you theenk I am Quetzalcoatl?"

Rowdy told him about their capture by Trimble's vaqueros and of the mysterious presence that had stampeded the Aztec crew from the vicinity of the cottonwood. "You showed up shortly after that," Rowdy added. "You came from below, of course, but you might have circled around. There was time enough."

Don Sebastian frowned. "Ees loco business," he decided. "Why ees Aztec god up here in Montana? How ees he getting along in cold winters I am hear tell about? Brr-rr!" He speared Rowdy with a glance. "What business breengs you to these parts, senor? Why ees this Gopher Kid try to keel you?"

"I don't answer that question," Rowdy mocked him. "You don't completely trust us, Alvarez, and I don't blame you. And since I don't know what your game is, I'm not completely trusting you. That's fair enough. But we made a bargain. You want to get inside Rancho Del Diablo, and so do we. I want a talk with Captain Buck Trimble. And I want to fetch Felicia out of there if she's inside and hankers to leave. As for that feathered J. B., I'm willing to pick it up for you, if I can. You saved our necks — a hat is cheap enough payment. But first we've got to get through that fence. And we'd better start figuring ways and means."

They were retracing the route Rowdy and Stumpy had followed when the Gopher Kid had fetched them from the vicinity of the gate. Often they were paralleling the high fence, and Rowdy looked across the creek at the many strands of wire speculatively.

"A fellow could crawl under that thing easy enough," he said. "Or he could climb over it. But I want a horse to tote me across those acres after I'm inside. If I had a pair of wire-cutters, I'd be inside faster than a hound dog can chase down a flea."

Don Sebastian patted his saddlebag. "The wire-cutters, they are here, senor," he said.

"Then what are we waiting for? There's not a soul around." Rowdy glanced beyond the fence; he could see a stretch of park-like country, grassy and tree-dotted, the land folding upward into deeper timber. Somewhere back in those hills, he supposed, were the ranch buildings of Trimble's spread. "Pass over those wire-cutters."

Don Sebastian looked sad. "Eet is not so simple," he said. "I, Don Sebastian Gregorio Jose de Ibarra y Alvarez, who have tried, tell you thees thing. Ees *indio* riders guarding thees fence day and night."

"I don't see any of them," Rowdy argued. "And the fence must run for miles and miles. How could every foot of it be watched all the time? How many riders has Trimble got?"

"Meellions!"

"Millions?"

"A hundred, perhaps," Don Sebastian amended.

"There were about twenty with the Gopher Kid," Rowdy recalled. "But I'll bet they're back at the bunkhouse right now, hiding their heads under blankets. You never saw such a scared bunch of jiggers. Once we're through the fence, we can get into timber shortly and hide ourselves. Even a hundred riders couldn't comb us out if we're the least bit lucky."

"They watch with the — what you call them? — field glasses," Don Sebastian explained. "Right now they watch us. When we use the wire-cutters, they come queek."

Frowning, Rowdy fell into a brown study, riding in silence for many minutes. "We can't wait around for all those Indians to die of old age," he finally announced. "But there are more ways to kill a cat than shooting it nine times with the same cannon. I've got a plan. It may not work, but it's worth a try. We'll head into the timber on the slope where we can't be seen from inside the fence, and we'll split up. You know the country fairly well, Alvarez?"

Don Sebastian nodded.

"I'll stay hereabouts," Rowdy said. "You and Stumpy wiggle your way through the woods and get across the road to the ranch and move along the fence a mile or so to the west. You should be able to put that much distance between you by early afternoon. Then the two of you separate, one going about a half-mile farther west. When you're all set, the one nearest the road can start his gun banging. Keep under cover, but raise all the fuss you can. That should bring the riders in that vicinity crowding to the fence."

"They will come pronto," Don Sebastian agreed.

"About that time, the other one of you can start lambasting the sky farther west. They won't want to leave one of you to go and investigate the other, so they'll probably send for more riders. I'm not expecting to be able to draw all of them to your vicinity, but at least they'll think they've got a heap of excitement over your way. About that time I'll chance cutting the fence and heading through here. Probably I'll run into trouble. But at least whatever men you toll to where you are won't be on my neck."

"Ees good plan," Don Sebastian decided after due consideration. "But ees getting only *one* hombre through the fence. That hombre should be me. I weel stay here, senors, and you weel raise the fuss on the other side of the gate."

"Nothing doing," Rowdy said flatly. "I made a bargain, but I didn't agree that you'd completely run the show. There's a chance for one of us to get inside — damn' little chance of all of us making it. That one's going to be *me,* mister. If I can lay my hands on that feathered hat, I won't forget you. But that's as far as I promised to string along."

Don Sebastian considered this in grave silence, his eyes probing Rowdy. Then he shrugged a shrug that was wholly Latin. "Very well, senor," he said. "I shall go with thees partner of yours and make the beeg fuss."

"Not so fast, you jiggers," Stumpy said sternly. "What's wrong with *me* staying here to cut the fence? I've got as much right to that chore as you have, Rowdy."

"That's so," Rowdy agreed. "No use arguing about it. Let's put it on a fair and square basis." He fished into his pocket and found a four-bit piece, sent it arching into the air, caught it and slapped it against the back of his hand. "Heads, Stumpy?"

"Tails," Stumpy countered obstinately.

"Too bad," Rowdy murmured, giving him a peek at the coin before he pocketed it.

They had been angling along the slope all this while, burying themselves deeper into the timber. They could no longer see the fence and thus felt themselves beyond any eyes on the far side of the wire. Rowdy extended his hand toward Don Sebastian. "The wire-cutters," Rowdy said. "And if you've any grub to spare, you might leave me a little."

Don Sebastian somewhat reluctantly passed over the wire-cutters and delved into his saddlebag for food which he also passed along.

"I'll hunker right here," Rowdy said. "I should be able to hear your guns when you start the hullabaloo. You won't be so far away in miles, even though it will take you a little time to get across that road. So long, now. And good luck."

Stumpy frowned at his partner. "You take keer of yourself, Rowdy," he said sternly.

"If I have trouble getting out again, and we lose track of each other, we can meet at Halfway House," Rowdy said. "Don't worry about me. Buck Trimble's on our side, and once I get to him I'll be safe. The Gopher Kid just takes his job too serious, that's all."

"Adios, senor," said Don Sebastian. "*Va ya con Dios*. I shall make the beeg fuss for you."

The two rode onward, the timber soon concealing them from Rowdy's sight, Stumpy looking back till the last, and after that Rowdy yawned, dismounted, hobbled his horse and unsaddled the mount, spreading the blanket upon the ground. Seating himself, he prepared for a lengthy vigil. He'd had very little sleep since coming to the Bearclaw country, but his thoughts kept him awake now, many unanswered questions spinning around in his head. Karst, for instance. Had the leader of the Shootin' Soreheads seen that Rowdy and Stumpy had ended up as prisoners of the Gopher Kid? Not likely. Karst had been in full flight then. Probably Karst thought the vaqueros had come roaring out of the ranch to protect the partners. Karst was doubtless now positively convinced that Rowdy was an employee of Rancho Del Diablo.

And Rowdy was, considering the thousand dollars he packed in his boot. But to work for Rancho Del Diablo, you had first to reach the boss and find out what manner of work he had in mind, and that, so far, had been an impossible chore in itself. Rowdy sighed and began dozing.

Intermittently he awoke, gazing at the sun and gauging the time. When high noon had come and gone, he worked his way through the timber afoot to a point where he could look out at the high fence and the country beyond it. No riders were in evidence. He stood looking for a long, long while, and, after an interminable wait, a group of vaqueros, a half-dozen in number, came patrolling the wire. They rode along at a steady trot, rifles across their laps, and vanished from sight where a clump of distant trees crowded to the wire.

Rowdy returned to the blanket and slept again. This time he was awakened by the distant rattle of gun-fire, the sound shaking asunder the thin silence of the high country. Stumpy and Don Sebastian! Coming to a stand, Rowdy saddled his horse and stood beside the mount, listening intently, waiting. Ten minutes crept by, fifteen, twenty. Only one gun had been banging, but now others were speaking as well; and Rowdy smiled grimly. Somebody had been fetched to the fence.

Still he waited, letting another fifteen minutes creep by. Then he mounted and rode boldly down the slope, pausing in the last of the thicker timber and having a look ahead. The fence was no more than a hundred yards beyond, the many strands of barbed wire glinting in the sunlight. No riders rode beyond it — not within Rowdy's range of vision anyway.

The guns were still banging far to the west, so many of them that it sounded as though a miniature war was in progress. Riding out of the timber, Rowdy splashed through the creek and approached the fence. Close to the wire, he sat his saddle, looking beyond. Still no one was in sight. He took the wire-cutters from his saddlebag and snipped a strand, and the taut wire, severed, went *zing-g-g!* He cut another strand and another, pausing between each for a searching look beyond, but nothing stirred. Finally, the last strand was severed, and he forced his mount through the opening thus made.

Rowdy drew a deep breath. He was inside Rancho Del Diablo, and the entry had been so easy that it was somehow terrifying.

CHAPTER VIII

RANCHO DEL DIABLO

A decided anticipatory itch between his shoulder blades, Rowdy rode warily, as nervous as a barefooted man in a blizzard, and so convinced was he that bullets would shortly be boring at him that he was almost disappointed when peace continued to reign within Rancho Del Diablo. At least in his immediate vicinity. The guns were still banging far to the west, but the sound was beginning to dwindle. Probably Don Sebastian and Stumpy, convinced that they'd given Rowdy sufficient time to make his entry, were withdrawing, their work completed. Rowdy began looking for cover.

He was paralleling the fence on the inside, heading for the clump of trees which had swallowed the patrolling vaqueros he'd seen not so long ago. In the trees, he sat his saddle for a good ten minutes, then spying another clump of trees a half-mile from the fence, he ventured out into the open and headed for the thicker timber. Sooner or later riders were going to find where the fence had been cut, and then the hue and cry would be raised. Rowdy's idea was to make himself as scarce as possible in the meantime.

Riding along, he lost some of his tense wariness and fell to admiring the terrain he traversed. This Rancho Del Diablo was the sort of paradise to which only good cows could hope to aspire; the grass was an endless carpet, and yonder hills provided shelter when the winter winds blew, and there was water a-plenty. Rowdy crossed a meandering creek three times before he reached the clump of trees which was his objective, and he judged the stream to be a tributary of Bearclaw Creek. Yes, Rancho Del Diablo was all a cattleman could ask for, and, remembering that this feudal domain had once been many ranches, welded into one by Buck Trimble's lust for power and land, Rowdy could understand why Abel Karst and the other dispossessed ranchers had stayed to make their fight. He could even sympathise with the Shootin' Soreheads.

He saw cattle grazing at a distance and judged them to be good, blooded stock. This was calf-branding time, and Rowdy, reflecting that a certain number of Trimble's vaqueros must be busy with the spring round-up, decided this factor was in his favour. Doubtless the fence-riders were limited in numbers to what they were at less busy seasons, and thus it might be that much longer before the broken fence was discovered.

Into the second clump of trees, Rowdy reined short and sat his saddle, and this time he saw riders, far to the south-west, cutting diagonally overland, heading in a general northerly direction. He watched them until they were lost to his sight and guessed that they had been some of the party drawn to the fence by Don Sebastian and Stumpy. He sat here for a long time, then ate half the food the caballero had left with him. Venturing to the creek, he had a drink.

An hour later, growing jumpy from inactivity, he caught up his grazing horse and headed north-west. He had to hump over a rise of land, and he reconnoitred from this ridge, seeing nothing to alarm him, seeing only another stretch of park-like land with the same serpentine creek crawling across it. Reaching timber again, he rested his saddle, and now he made out a spiral of smoke dangling in the thin mountain air to the north-west. This, he judged, marked the ranch-buildings of Trimble's spread, but the buildings were shut from his view by another rise of land.

Rowdy glanced at the lowering sun.

Somewhere about those buildings would be Captain Buck Trimble, soldier of fortune — the real Buck Trimble, not the impostor who'd appeared in Bearclaw wearing the feathered sombrero — and Rowdy's mission was to reach Trimble. But he'd need darkness to cover him when he approached those buildings, and now he awaited the darkness with as much patience as he could command. The dusk came at long last, the shadows flowing down from the hills and the greyness making all things murky. But still Rowdy bided his time.

Once he thought he saw riders off at a distance, to the south, but he couldn't be sure. He waited, ears strained for the nearing beat of hoofs, a betraying jingle of bit chains. But if there'd been riders, they must have veered away from him, for he heard nothing but the normal sounds of this mountain country — the raucous call of crows, the incessant babbling of the creek, the scurrying of unseen rodents.

When the deep darkness came, he moved out of the timber and began climbing the gentle slope which stood between him and his destination. The moon showed itself over the eastern hills, seemed to hesitate in its ascent as though it feared Rancho Del Diablo, then lifted into view. And thus when

Rowdy finally stood at the top of the slope, there was moonlight to bathe the buildings in the open land below him. And Rowdy looking, drew in his breath in astonishment.

He'd expected the citadel of Buck Trimble to be lavish, but he'd expected, too, that the buildings would conform to the usual architecture of the country. Montana was a land of log and frame, and in the mountains a man expected log. But those buildings below glistened white in the first moonlight and stood square and sturdy, no gables lifting, and suddenly Rowdy understood. Adobe! They were made of adobe, Mexican fashion. Rowdy had gleaned a little advance information about Rancho Del Diablo both in Miles City and since arriving in the Bearclaw country, but he wasn't prepared for this.

He might have been looking at some hacienda on the outskirts of Santa Fe, or a wealthy rancho south of the turgid Rio Grande. There was the big house with a wall surrounding it, and outside the wall stood several smaller buildings, square in design, and a scattering of adobe corrals. Ancient trees cast dark shadows upon buildings and wall. He was seeing a bit of Mexico transplanted to a far northern land, and the sight was staggering. True, old Fort Benton on the distant Missouri had been built of adobe, but those sun-dried bricks were not in general usage. Captain Buck Trimble had fetched manana-land to Montana.

But there was no percentage in sitting a saddle with his lowered jaw flapping, so Rowdy, his first surprise passing, moved on down the slope towards the buildings, circling to approach the main one from the rear. Lamplight made yellow rectangles of grilled windows in the second storey. A hundred yards from the main building, he dismounted, leaving his mount ground-anchored with trailing reins, and ventured forward on foot.

The adobe wall surrounding the huge main building was ten feet high, and a wrought-iron gate centred this wall to the rear. The gate was ajar, but a man hunkered near it, crouched down with his back to the wall, his cone-shaped sombrero tipped forward over his eyes, a cigarette alive in his face, a rifle draped across his lap. Rowdy paused, debating with himself. He might march boldly to this guard and demand an audience with Captain Trimble, and he might thus be taken directly to the master of Rancho Del Diablo. But these native retainers of the place seemed to receive their orders from the Gopher Kid, who had proved himself as short on hospitality as a rattlesnake. Possibly this one at the gate had been among the group who'd sat saddles beneath the cottonwood that morning, waiting with glittering eyes for Rowdy and Stumpy to die.

Edging into the shadows, Rowdy got his back to the wall and began inching along it toward the sentry. For Rowdy, weighing the factors, had decided he would continue the role of invader until he stood in the presence of Trimble himself. He moved as silently as he could; the sentry might have been slumbering except that he raised a hand from time to time to remove the cigarette from his mouth. Each time the man moved, Rowdy froze immobile, but at last he hovered over the man. Some instinct must have aroused the sentry at that moment, some sensation of danger. He looked up and saw Rowdy, and his hands closed tightly on the rifle. Rowdy brought the barrel of his six-shooter down hard across that cone-shaped sombrero.

The sentry sagged into a shapeless heap with no more than a moan, and instantly Rowdy was tugging at him, drawing the unconscious form along the wall to the shadows banked beside a stone watering trough. The gate was now open to Rowdy, but he realised that other guards might be standing between him and Trimble, so he'd decided on a ruse. Stripping the sentry, Rowdy peeled out of his own garb, dropping his foxed trousers and pearl-buttoned shirt in a heap. When he had dressed again, he stood in cotton trousers and coarse shirt, a battered straw sombrero on his head, a greasy serape thrown over his shoulder.

He used his discarded neckerchief to bind the sentry's hands behind him; a bit of rope that had served as the vaquero's belt now served to lash his ankles. In the cotton trousers Rowdy found an extremely dirty bandanna, and with a wry grimace he thrust this into the sentry's mouth. Thrusting his six-shooter into the front of his borrowed shirt, Rowdy returned to the gate and lifted the sentry's rifle and stood it against the wall, back in the shadows.

Now he shuffled through the gate and found himself in a tile-paved courtyard where a fountain tinkled musically. Above him reared the house, a huge structure with two angling wings giving the building the shape of an incomplete letter E. A balcony ran above, the grilled windows of the second storey showing behind it. As Rowdy swept his eyes along the balcony, he saw the girl for the second time. She stood upon the balcony, clad in a long white dress topped by a mantilla, her face sad, her face beautiful. She was looking directly down at him, and he said, "Felicia!" softly, under his breath.

He wondered if she recognised him but knew that this could not be so. She'd only had that one other glimpse of him, the storm-swept night when she'd signalled so frantically from the window of Halfway House in the lightning's flare. He tore his eyes from her now lest his interest arouse her suspicion, for he was suddenly remembering that he was in the guise of a lowly *mestizo* who did not look upon grand ladies with anything but servitude in their glance. He moved forward across the courtyard.

A door opened and a splash of light was thrown across the tiling. Rowdy saw that the door gave from a kitchen. Several figures were in the courtyard, moving with seeming aimlessness but apparently occupied with their own business. And then Rowdy spied two more sentries of the like of the one he'd so recently rendered unconscious. They were seated on either side of a dark doorway leading into one of the wings, and as he watched, a native woman, shapeless beneath a shawl, approached this door, spoke a few words and was admitted. Shortly thereafter she came out of the door; the room beyond seemed to be only dimly lighted. A few minutes later a man — one of the vaqueros from his garb — approached and was also admitted. He, too, spent no more than a very brief time inside.

Rowdy's curiosity was thoroughly aroused. His first supposition had been that this was the rear entrance to Captain Trimble's own quarters and thus was guarded. The impostor in Bearclaw had said that Karst's crew would shoot Trimble on sight, and thus Trimble might take more than ordinary precautions to keep himself safe. And Trimble, in the letter he'd left with the hotel clerk in Bearclaw, had indicated that he felt his life in danger. But the rank and file of Trimble's retainers wouldn't be paying these many visits to their master, and their comings and goings gave the lie to Rowdy's first theory.

Shuffling about the courtyard, Rowdy toyed with the notion of approaching the sentries and asking a mumbled permission to enter. But the chance was too strong that he'd betray himself. He could speak passable Spanish, but he was remembering that Trimble's vaqueros had a tongue of their own — possibly the Nahuatl dialect of the original Aztecs, which the Bearclaw impostor had mentioned. No, it would be far too risky for Rowdy to open his mouth unnecessarily.

Inspired, he turned and headed back towards the gate, but instead of dodging through it, he eased into the shadows and began following the wall on the inside. Soon he was on the other side of the wing that had aroused his interest, and here he found small windows set in the wall of the wing. Most of these windows were dark, but one glowed dimly, and, making a mental calculation, Rowdy judged this one to be the window of the guarded room. He approached it carefully, raised himself on tiptoes and peered inside. And for the second time that night he was stunned at what he saw.

The room was small and illuminated only by candles, and it was almost bare of furnishings. Inside were two other sentries, standing wooden-like along the wall near the door, and as Rowdy looked, the door opened and another shawled native woman entered. She crossed quickly and knelt down before a raised dais at the end of the room nearest the window. She was here only a moment, praying apparently, and then she departed, one of the sentries coming to life long enough to open the door for her. But what held Rowdy's startled eyes was the sheet-draped figure upon the dais, candles burning smokily at head and feet.

"He was a big man, red-faced, and had a white moustache and a beak of a nose, and a regular mane of white hair . . ." the Bearclaw desk-clerk had said of Captain Buck Trimble. And such a description aptly fitted the lifeless figure upon the dais.

And now Rowdy was remembering many things and understanding them. Captain Trimble writing: "I've reason to fear that my life is in danger . . ." The Gopher Kid giggling this morning and saying, "So you're going to work for Captain Trimble. Well, it won't be long. It won't be long," saying this when Rowdy's horse had taken a step and it had looked as though Rowdy were shortly to die.

Rowdy had supposed that Buck Trimble had feared for his life because of Abel Karst and his crew and their sworn intent to kill the man who'd dispossessed them. But Trimble hadn't died by the hands of the Shootin' Soreheads, for Karst had certainly not known of Trimble's passing, at least not yesterday when Karst had talked to Rowdy and Stumpy in the cabin calaboose. And Trimble had been dead for more than a day, if Rowdy was any judge. The wax-like figure on the dais had the look of having been embalmed.

His head whirling, Rowdy stepped back from the window. And at that precise moment he heard the wild outcry beyond the wall. The sentry! The fellow had come awake and rid himself of the gag Rowdy had so hastily stuffed in his mouth! Feet were thudding along outside the wall, bare feet and booted feet — the feet of men drawn by the sentry's outcry. Quickly Rowdy hurried around into the courtyard, and the courtyard was swarming now with men. Doors were banging everywhere. Rowdy cast a hasty glance upward; Felicia was no longer on the balcony.

Rowdy's thought was to mix with the crowd and become part of it, finding anonymity among numbers, but someone jarred against him in hasty passage, knocking Rowdy's borrowed sombrero to the tiled paving. Rowdy bent to pick up the cone-shaped hat and was bending when a door opened nearby and the light fell upon him. The man who'd careened into him was mumbling something that sounded more like a curse than an apology, and now this man shouted in the weird tongue of his kind and fell upon Rowdy. Frantically Rowdy fought to reach the gun inside his shirt, but many men were coming, fetched by the shouts of the one with whom Rowdy struggled, and many hands fastened upon Rowdy.

He was pressed down by the combined weight of his adversaries, and his arms were pinioned, and he gave up the struggle, knowing he could not prevail against such odds.

CHAPTER IX

KILLED WITH KINDNESS

The sages have said that he who fights and runs away shall live to fight another day, but Rowdy Dow was in the sad situation of being able to neither fight nor run. A quarter of a ton of Aztecs heaped upon him, he was finding it difficult even to hoist an eyebrow, and he was unceremoniously hauled to his feet, and his gun was wrenched away from him. It made a bleak and bitter moment. He had successfully penetrated to the very heart of Rancho Del Diablo, but his invasion had been planned to bring him into the sanctuary of Captain Buck Trimble's presence. But Captain Trimble lay dead in a nearby room, and Rowdy could expect to find no other friend on this sinister rancho.

Around him his captors were babbling in that strange tongue of theirs, with just enough Spanish to it to convey a smattering of sense to Rowdy. The question seemed to be just what to do with the prisoner, and there was mention of *El Topo* — the Gopher Kid, Rowdy judged — and several references to a Senor Turk. Rowdy's attention riveting upon that name, he remembered a Gideon Turk who'd been mentioned in Bearclaw, both by the impostor with the feathered sombrero and by Abel Karst. Turk, the lawyer — the man who'd helped Buck Trimble forge this stolen empire. Turk, the right-hand man of Captain Trimble. Turk would likely be in charge now that Trimble was dead.

And it was to Gideon Turk that Rowdy was being taken. They hustled him across the tiled paving to a door giving into the main part of the building, and as that door swung open a man stood framed there, a tall, cadaverous man in rusty black, the feathered sombrero perched upon his head — that same man whom Rowdy had twice met before — once violently in the darkness of Halfway House, once peaceably when Gideon Turk had appeared in Bearclaw and pretended to be Captain Buck Trimble. For this was the impostor who'd made Rowdy a proposition that was to have sent the partners to distant Mexico City.

And now, for the first time, Rowdy knew him to be Gideon Turk, and his surprise was as great as Turk's as they came face to face once again. Turk falling back, Rowdy was marched down a hallway into a huge room lavishly furnished with carved mahogany, a room out of Old Spain. Glittering candelabra threw soft light upon expensive Navaho rugs; and the oil painting framed upon the walls looked as though they might each be worth a fortune. A suit of armour that had belonged to a conquistador stood in one corner. All in all, it was as fancy a place for a man to die as Rowdy could have expected to find in a year of riding.

Rowdy's captors were babbling again, Gideon Turk listening intently, and then Turk barked a command in the same alien tongue; and Rowdy, to his surprise, felt the hands of his captors fall away from him.

"My profound apologies, Mr. Dow," said Gideon Turk. "This incident is very regrettable. But I can only remind you that I mentioned in Bearclaw that I have many enemies. Consequently my vaqueros are more zealous than discriminating." His eyes flicked over Rowdy's borrowed garb from the cotton trousers to the greasy serape. "You'll have to concede that you hardly look the part of a visitor such as I, Captain Trimble, might be expecting. And I'm told that you assaulted a sentry in order to get the garb you're wearing."

Out of all this, Rowdy sorted one fact that set his head to buzzing. Gideon Turk was still pretending to be Buck Trimble! And

Turk was apparently presuming that Rowdy hadn't guessed his true identity. Turk wanted to keep on playing games! And because Rowdy sensed that any indication on his own part that he was no longer fooled would change Turk's role from apologetic host to unmasked enemy, Rowdy was most willing to string along with the ruse.

"Sorry about having to clout the fellow at the gate," he said. "But when I tried to come to this ranch peaceably, I nearly got hanged!"

"Sit down. Sit down," Turk urged with a wave of his hand toward a high-backed chair. Another gesture cleared the room of the vaqueros who'd fetched Rowdy here. Rowdy seated, Turk said, "Am I to presume that your coming here means you changed your mind about that little mission I mentioned?"

"That was the notion," Rowdy said, happy to have such a motive to seize upon. "The more I got thinking about it, the more I realised that Mexico City pasear might have its points. But Abel Karst locked me and my partner up in his calaboose because he knew you'd visited us. After we managed to break out, we had to spend a little time dodging the Shootin' Soreheads. With Karst convinced that I was in cahoots with you,

Captain, it seemed like I might just as well be."

"Your partner? What's his name? Frumpy Grumpit? He's not with you?"

"I'm getting to that," Rowdy said. "We reached Rancho Del Diablo this morning, with Karst hard after us. Your segundo, the Gopher Kid, came roaring out with his vaqueros and ran Karst down the road. But afterwards the Kid perched us on our horses under a cottonwood and was set to let us do an air dance. We managed to untie each other, and after that Stumpy lit out. He'd had enough of Rancho Del Diablo and its hospitality. If I take the Mexico City trip for you, I take it alone."

"I see." Turk's eyes narrowed thoughtfully. "Again I owe you an apology, though I realise how inadequate any apology must sound. Let us say that the Gopher Kid is an extremely capable man when it comes to handling our savage riders or our cattle. Let us say that his merits along those lines are so great that I've been forced to overlook certain tendencies of his toward homicide. He saw you and your partner as strangers at the gate, and he acted in my best interests — according to his light. Doubtless he thought that your being pursued by Karst was a ruse to gain you entrance to the ranch.

The Kid is still somewhere out yonder attending to his duties. I haven't seen him to-day. When he reports here, he'll be severely reprimanded!"

"I'd like a hand in that!" Rowdy said darkly.

Turk smiled. "And deprive me of an extremely able segundo? I'm afraid not, Dow. Ah, what's this?" One of the vaqueros had entered, his arms laden with Rowdy's clothes. These were dumped upon the floor at Turk's feet, and Turk said, "Your garb, eh? There's a screen in the corner. I'm sure you'll feel more comfortable in your own clothes. And you must be hungry. I'll have food fetched while you're dressing."

Shrugging, Rowdy picked up his clothes and went behind the indicated screen. When he emerged a few minutes later, wearing his foxed trousers and pearl-buttoned shirt, Turk was coming from one of the other rooms after having apparently issued orders for food. Rowdy said pointedly, "All dressed up except for my gun. One of your boys plucked it off me."

"You'll need no gun within these walls," Turk said with a placating smile. A native woman appeared, bearing a tray which she placed upon a long, ornate table which centred the room. Turk himself moved Rowdy's high-backed chair to the table. "Eat, Mr. Dow," he urged. "We can continue our talk as you do."

Rowdy fell upon the food, automatically recalling a quotation much abused by the press. Condemned men always ate hearty meals. This little game was verging upon a cat-and-mouse affair — Turk's refusal to give him his gun was significant — and Rowdy was growing increasingly wary. Still, there were questions he wanted to ask; but he bided his time.

"So," Turk said, "after escaping from the Kid and having a parting of the ways with Mr. Stumple, you decided to try and get in touch with me anyway? I'm curious to know how you got through the fence."

"I cut it," Rowdy frankly admitted.

"*You cut it!* Where?"

Rowdy told him, making the location as vague as possible. Turk clapped his hands, and one of the stone-faced vaqueros bobbed through a doorway. To this man Turk spoke in the alien tongue, and the man disappeared. The fence, Rowdy judged, was going to be fixed mighty soon.

"The rest of it you know," Rowdy said. "I waited till dark, clouted the sentry, and got into the courtyard. I tangled my twine, had a tussle, and was fetched to you. It was a long way around Robin Hood's barn, but I made it. You said you'd tell me more about that Aztec sword if I'd take on the job of getting it."

Turk nudged back the feathered sombrero, and Rowdy wondered if he wore it night and day. "Ah, yes, of course," Turk said. "A bit of brandy after your meal? We have some Napoleon 1814. Come, I'll have it served in the library. We'll be more comfortable there."

"The library!" Rowdy said aloud and started in spite of himself, remembering the note Captain Trimble had left with the Bearclaw hotel clerk — the note and the thousand dollars. Both the note and the money were still in his boot-top.

"This way," said Gideon Turk and ushered Rowdy through one of the several archways giving off the big room. They came into a low-ceilinged room whose walls were solidly lined with books. A small brass-bound lamp burned upon a centring table, and large, comfortable chairs were strewn about. Rowdy seated, Turk clapped his hands again; the same native woman who had served the food appeared and was given an order and departed. Shortly she returned, this time bearing a tray upon which stood a brandy bottle and two goblets.

"Your pleasure?" Turk asked, tilting the bottle.

"A short snort," said Rowdy. He took the glass, then watched carefully. Turk poured himself some of the brandy and unhesitantly lifted his own glass to his lips. He took a sip, then proposed a belated toast: "To the sword of the Montezumas. And to your success in getting it for me."

"Mud in your eye," said Rowdy.

"A cigar," Turk urged, opening a lacquered box upon the table. "These are Havana imports, dipped in wine."

"I'm being killed with kindness," Rowdy murmured, taking the proffered weed. "Now, about that sword —"

"As I told you," Turk said, "I have a collection of Aztec curios. But perhaps it would be best if we waited till morning before I show it to you. You've obviously had a trying day."

Rowdy blew a smoke-ring. "Speaking of things Aztec, those boys who were with the Gopher Kid to-day started stirring the dust when one of them thought he saw someone called Quetzalcoatl. You mentioned in Bearclaw that the jigger was an Aztec god your vaqueros had claimed to have seen here in Montana. Frankly, I thought that was a windy worthy of my partner, who strings some tall ones. But those boys were really pawing the sod to-day."

Turk sighed, leaning back in his chair and sipping at the brandy. "When you deal with a primitive people, you deal with superstition, Dow. You and I are intelligent, enlightened men, and we know very well that Quetzalcoatl does not stalk the Bearclaw country. Yet my riders claim to have seen him several times recently. How is that to be accounted for? Self-hypnotism? A suggestion becoming contagious?"

"Now, me," said Rowdy, "I wouldn't know Quetzalcoatl if he walked in and borrowed the makings."

"Quetzalcoatl was probably the best known of the Aztec gods," Turk explained. "Far less cruel than most of their deities, he did not demand human sacrifices, though his priests were given to piercing their tongues and ears and spreading the blood upon the mouths of the idols. Both in Mexico and among the Mayans, Quetzalcoatl was considered as the god of light, of the sun, of thunder, of winds, and of the cardinal points of the compass. He had many names, and there are many legends concerning him."

"Sounds like Stumpy's Uncle Tio," Rowdy remarked.

"Quetzalcoatl was always represented as a white man with a full beard, garbed in a black robe bordered with white crosses. The Mayans, too, had a Plumed Serpent god, Kukulcan, who was also represented as a bearded man. My personal opinion, which is also borne by some very learned men, is that the myths were the result of the actual arrival of some European centuries ago. A Viking, perhaps. One legend is that he arrived in a weird, winged ship in the vicinity of what is now Vera Cruz. He's supposed to have taught the Aztecs many arts."

"He was plenty helpful as far as I was concerned," Rowdy conceded.

"He prophesied, Mr. Dow, that white warriors would eventually arrive from across the ocean and overthrow the Aztecs and enforce another religion. But he also prophesied that he would one day return and lead the Aztecs back to their original faith. All of this sounds far-fetched, I know, yet it is a matter of history that the Aztecs were not at all astonished when Cortez arrived on the shores of Mexico."

"And what became of old Quetzy?" Rowdy asked. "Had he lit out before that?"

"There are many myths regarding his departure. One has it that he cast himself on a funeral pyre, his ashes flew upward and were changed to birds. Another tale is that he grew disgusted with the perversion of the Aztecs' faith and departed on a magic raft of intertwined serpents."

Rowdy yawned. "And where do you place your betting money, Captain?"

Turk smiled ruefully. "Your tendency to scoff is only natural," he said. "I fear that I bore you, and you are weary enough. I'll have you conducted to one of the bedrooms. In the morning we can resume our talk and get down to more pertinent business."

But there was one question Rowdy wished mightily to ask, and he risked it now. Looking around the room, he said, "You live well, Captain. Mighty well. Too bad you have nobody to share all this with. Or am I mistaken? Are you a married man? I thought I saw a grand lady on the balcony just before your boys decided to flatten me out."

Turk tilted the brandy bottle again, his eyes lowered to the task. "You must have been mistaken, Mr. Dow. There are no women here but the native women who are the wives of some of my vaqueros and serve about the place in various capacities. Perhaps it was one of those you saw."

"Likely," Rowdy said lazily and arose, stretching himself.

Turk clapped his hands. "A servant will show you to your bed," he said.

Rowdy nodded, seemingly the most indolent man in the world but hiding a tenseness that made his nerves strum. He'd been dragged into this friendless house expecting to die; instead he'd been dined and wined and entertained. Yet the feeling had never left him that he stood in danger. Gideon Turk was keeping up the pretence of being Captain Trimble for a reason; Turk was playing a cat-and-mouse game of some sort, and the game was not yet finished. But luck had attended Rowdy so far tonight, and he decided to press his luck.

The native woman appeared to listen to an order from Turk, and Rowdy stepped towards the biggest door. Stretching himself again, he yawned noisily and said, "Mind if I take a book along to read myself to sleep?" Without waiting for an answer, he reached for a book — the third book from the left on the fourth shelf from the floor — the book in which Captain Trimble had left written instructions for him.

"I would never have guessed you to be a scholar, Mr. Dow," said Gideon Turk with a smile. "You've chosen a ponderous tome."

"The heavier the book, the sooner I'll

sleep," said Rowdy. "Good night, Captain. See you in the morning."

"Good night," said Gideon Turk.

CHAPTER X

SO FAR AND NO FARTHER

Rowdy trailing behind her, the native woman, a lamp held high, led the way up a wide stair to a hall where five horses might have passed abreast, a hall so thickly carpeted that Rowdy had the sensation of wading rather than walking. Huge, ornate doors gave off this hall, and Rowdy was quick to note that a vaquero squatted before one, his sombrero down over his eyes, his general appearance much like the sentry's who'd been posted at the gate, except that this guard had no rifle. The man scarcely looked up as Rowdy was escorted past him. Several doors beyond, the native woman moved into a room.

"Here, senor," she said.

She placed the lamp atop a carved, rosewood bureau and Rowdy whistled softly, his eyes sweeping a canopied bed and several pieces of stiff furniture of an earlier period. A wide stone fireplace stood at the end of the bedroom, a painting of the Madonna gave its benediction from an alabaster wall. Here was enough comfort to last a man a month of Sundays, and Rowdy, still clutching the book he'd taken from the library, wondered if he was to be provided with a silk nightgown and a tasselled cap.

"Eef you require something," said the woman, "ees bellrope beside the bed."

"I'll struggle along," said Rowdy.

The woman nodded and withdrew from the room, leaving the lamp on the bureau. A screen stood in one corner, and Rowdy quickly had a look behind it. Nothing there. He turned the heavy tome over in his hands, holding it to the lamplight, and whistled again. The book was in Latin! Small wonder Gideon Turk had been startled by Rowdy's choice of reading matter! The question was whether Turk had been more than startled. Had he been suspicious?

Flipping the pages, Rowdy came upon a sealed envelope which apparently contained many sheets of flimsy paper, and he drew in his breath triumphantly. Here was the document Buck Trimble had meant for his hands. He was about to run his thumb under the flap when there was a gentle tapping at the door. Thrusting the envelope inside his shirt, Rowdy said, "Come in."

The native woman bore a tray upon which sat a goblet filled with brandy, and this she placed beside the bed. "Ees nightcap," she explained. "Compliments of El Capitan. Ees to bring the sleep if the reading keep you awake."

"Now that was mighty thoughtful of him," said Rowdy. He extended the book. "You can take this back to El Capitan with *muchas gracias*. Tell him I made a mistake. The only Latin I savvy is pig Latin."

Her face expressionless, she took the book and left the room again. Rowdy glanced at the brandy. Had Gideon Turk indeed been suspicious? And, if so, would returning the book allay his suspicions, convincing him that Rowdy had taken the tome without realising its worthlessness to him as reading matter? Obviously Turk had known nothing about the envelope or he would have removed it long ago.

But the matter of the book was only part of the greater mystery surrounding Gideon Turk's attitude. If the man had Rowdy pegged as an enemy, Turk could have had the intruder killed at the time of Rowdy's capture. Instead, Turk had chosen to wine and dine him. Did Turk really crave an Aztec sword from a Mexico City museum, and, thinking Rowdy to be unsuspecting of his real identity intend to dispatch Rowdy on the long pasear? Rowdy had his own theory concerning that Mexican trip, but as yet he had no proof to confirm it. And now, suddenly, Rowdy was stiffening with alarm, for something had become as plain as the nose on Stumpy Grampis's face.

Turk had been concerned as to what had fetched Rowdy into the heart of Rancho Del Diablo, and what was equally important, how Rowdy had managed to gain entry into the guarded ranch. Of course! And, since dead men made poor hands at answering questions, Turk had allowed Rowdy to live. More than that, Turk had pretended to be Buck Trimble, made apologies, spread hospitality with a lavish hand — and thereby placed himself in a position to ask questions. The game had been to lull Rowdy's suspicions. Turk, Rowdy recalled, hadn't extended his hospitality to the point of returning Rowdy's gun!

All of which added up to the fact that if Rowdy were now guessing right, Turk had learned everything he'd wanted to learn, and therefore Rowdy's danger had really just begun. An assassin in the night? Perhaps. A sleeping potion in the nightcap to leave Rowdy completely at the mercy of a nocturnal killer? Rowdy sniffed at the brandy. He couldn't be sure. Grinning wryly, he lifted the goblet and opened the door slightly. People stirred downstairs, but this second storey was wrapped in silence. Striding boldly into the hall, Rowdy walked toward the sentry who crouched before one of the doors.

"Your name, senor?" Rowdy asked in border Spanish.

"Pedro Montez."

"Here is something to make your vigil less tedious, Pedro. I have had enough brandy for one night."

Suspicion lighted the sentry's eyes, flared briefly and died as Rowdy held the brandy near enough to Pedro's nose to give him a whiff of it. A brown hand extended, grasped the goblet, tilted it.

"Gracias," said the sentry, returning the empty goblet and drawing his hand across his chin.

"Think nothing of it, old horse," said Rowdy and returned to his room.

Extinguishing the lamp, he kept the door slightly ajar and posted himself by it. A few minutes later Gideon Turk passed down the hallway, looking neither to the left nor to the right; a door opened and closed a moment later, and Rowdy judged that Turk had retired for the night. The man had been wearing the feathered sombrero, and Rowdy was becoming more convinced that the hat never left Turk. Pressing an ear to the wall, Rowdy tried listening for any sounds from

Turk's room, but either the walls were too thick or Turk's room was too far removed from this one.

Now the great house was settling to silence. Lights were extinguished below, leaving the stairs and the upper hallway in darkness. The minutes crawled by and became a half-hour, and Rowdy ventured into the hall again. Thankful for those thick rugs, he stole toward Pedro Montez and found that worthy with his head between his knees, fast asleep, his breathing deep and steady. No normal sleep this; the brandy had indeed been drugged.

Whereupon Rowdy put his hand to the great door the sentry had so ineptly guarded. He knew full well whom he'd find inside, for he'd already guessed why one of the bedrooms had a sentry posted before it; and when he got into the room and closed the door, he prayed that Felicia wouldn't be awake to raise an alarm before she could realise that he'd come to her aid. This room was much like the one provided for him; it held the same straight-backed chairs and a canopied bed; and this he saw in the light of a single candle burning upon the rosewood bureau. And he also saw the girl sitting in the bed, the coverlet pulled to her chin, her long black hair spilling to her shoulders, her eyes big and afraid, the makings of a scream growing in them.

He got across the room in a bound and clamped his hand tightly over her mouth and bore her back against the pillows, shutting off any outcry before it could come. "I'm a friend!" he whispered urgently, putting his lips close to her ear. "I'm the man you signalled from the window of Halfway House night before last! I'm here to get you free! I'll take my hand away if you promise not to scream."

Her eyes still big, she managed to nod. He released his hand. "Sorry to have been rough," he said.

This was his first close look at her, and he saw that her eyes were brown and long-lashed. The fear was gone from them now.

"I remember you from that stormy night!" she said quickly. Her voice was soft and liquid and her speech had far less of a Spanish accent than he'd expected. "You startled me when you first crept in, just now. You found my message in the dust of the window-sill, senor?"

"I found it," he said. There were many questions he wanted to ask her, but this was neither the time nor the place for them. "Do you have clothes handy? Clothes for the trail?"

"I have riding garb in the closet."

"Then pile into it," Rowdy advised. "And hurry."

He put his back to her as she climbed out of the bed. Returning to the door, he opened it slightly and kept vigil while she delved into a closet and then hurried behind a screen. A few minutes later she stepped out, looking far less Latin in close-fitting riding-breeches, a soft silk shirt and an embroidered jacket.

"Do you know this house?" Rowdy demanded. "Can you find your way around it?"

"I've had the freedom of the hacienda," she said, "but I've been closely watched. All the servants know me by sight. Our path will be beset with difficulties."

"Difficulties," said Rowdy, "come a dime a dozen in this Bearclaw country. I've got a chore to do before I shed myself of this shebang. A promise to a galoot who kept my neck from being stretched. Do you know which room is Gideon Turk's?"

"Five doors down the hall, senor."

"I'll be right back," said Rowdy.

He eased into the hall; the sentry was now snoring slightly, and Rowdy felt a twinge of sympathy. Pedro Montez would likely get an earful on the subject of inefficiency come morning. Moving along the hall, Rowdy counted doors until he'd passed his own and come to the fifth, the one to Turk's room. The door gave to his touch, and blackness lay beyond it. Rowdy stood for a moment just within the room, listening intently, his eyes straining. Moonlight trickled feebly through a grilled window; he made out a canopied bed and the form within it, and then he drew in a long breath as he recognised the silhouette of the feathered sombrero on a nearby chair.

He grasped the sombrero, and for want of a better means of carrying it, placed it upon his head. He wished mightily for a gun and was sorry the drugged sentry had not been provided with one. Doubtless Turk would have a weapon handy. He debated as to whether to search the room, and was debating when Turk stirred, muttered, and turned over on his side.

Quickly Rowdy slid from the room. Coming back down the hall, he let himself into Felicia's room and found her waiting. She gazed in surprise at the sombrero he now wore, and said, "Ah, senor, not only are you brave, you are clever as well!"

"You think so?" Rowdy asked in surprise.

"You know that these *nativos* recognise the sombrero as a symbol of authority. It shall pass us out of this place." She took his hand. "Come."

He was willing enough to have her do the leading; she knew the hacienda far better than he did. Into the hall, she skirted Pedro Montez with a great deal more caution than was called for until Rowdy whispered, "Drugged!" They came down the stairs together, and again Rowdy was thankful for the thick carpeting. The lower floor was in complete darkness, but Rowdy sensed that the room in which they found themselves was the one where he'd first talked to Turk tonight. They moved across it, and Rowdy inadvertently careened into a chair, upsetting it.

"Damn!" he muttered.

A door opened, a splash of light falling into this room; and three native women peered from the opened doorway. It led from the kitchen, Rowdy judged. The three stared with more show of expression than Rowdy had ever detected in these misplaced Aztecs, their eyes lifting to the sombrero Rowdy wore; and they quietly closed the door.

"Damn!" Rowdy muttered again — this time with awe.

"Come!" Felicia urged, drawing Rowdy towards a doorway which he was sure led deeper into the hacienda. But to his astonishment, this gave into a short *galeria* that led to the tiled courtyard where the fountain splashed and the stars wheeled overhead — the rear courtyard in which he had been captured. Yonder, the two sentries were still posted before the room in the wing where Rowdy had seen the silent form that had been Captain Buck Trimble. A few vaqueros loitered in the courtyard. They had their look at the two who emerged from the house; they had their look at the feathered sombrero and fell back, making no move to stop the pair.

"This," Rowdy chuckled, "is like shooting fish in a rainbarrel." He glanced upward to the balcony and eyed the many windows. All of them were dark, which meant — Rowdy fervently hoped — that Gideon Turk was still bedded down, blissfully unaware that two guests of the ranch were making their departure. "Horses!" Rowdy whispered. "If we can only get ourselves aboard some horses."

"There is a stable built into the end of the far wing, senor," Felicia explained. "The private stable of the master of this horrible place. Many times I have watched the saddling from the balcony these last two days."

"Lead me to it," said Rowdy.

They moved unchallenged across the courtyard. Felicia had been absolutely correct in her assumption that the feathered sombrero would be a passport from this place, and Rowdy was now remembering the questions Stumpy had put to Gideon Turk in Bearclaw. Turk had explained that the sombrero was the equivalent of an Aztec feathered headdress and therefore a badge of authority in the minds of Rancho Del Diablo's vaqueros. Rowdy had taken all this with a grain of salt at the time. Now he was having a demonstration of the sombrero's powers.

Into the stable, they found half a dozen horses in stalls, and when Rowdy boldly lighted a lantern, he discovered one of the mounts to be his own. It must have been found where he'd left it and fetched here. Likewise his own saddle was here, hung upon a peg. Slapping the saddle on the mount, he said, "You take this cayuse, senorita. He's mine, and I know he's fast." He ran his eye over the other horses; they were all good stock, and he selected one which looked adequately long on both speed and bottom, and quickly got a saddle upon it. The lantern extinguished, they led the mounts out into the courtyard and toward the gate.

"It's closed for the night," Rowdy observed, peering ahead. "If you have a patron saint, senorita, pray that it's not locked."

Felicia's hand faltered to her throat. "I'm afraid it is, senor. That is why they are careless of keys inside the hacienda. With the gate locked at night, they need not fear that an enemy will gain the house."

"Somebody's got a key," Rowdy muttered. "One look at this hat and he'll probably fork it over. But who's our man?" Struck by another thought, he fumbled in his boot top and got the letter Trimble had left for him in Bearclaw, and he took from his shirt the documents he'd got from the book to-night. "Here," he said, handing the papers to Felicia. "We've got this far; the question is whether we'll get any farther. If we should get separated, hang on to these papers for me. You'll find the fence cut in yonder direction." He swept an arm to the south-east. "I'm hoping they haven't had time to patch it yet."

"Shhh!" she cautioned him, her hand tightening upon his arm. "Somebody is outside the gate, opening it!"

"Luck!" Rowdy exulted, then quickly changed his mind. He was peering hard and there was just enough moonlight to show him who stood beyond the ironwork, fumbling with a key. "The Gopher Kid!" he ejaculated, for it was indeed that buck-toothed little killer. "Senorita, we're just about to bump into one gent who doesn't give a whoop for Aztec tomfoolery. This sombrero won't mean a thing to him! Not when it's on *my* head!"

He was again wishing mightily for a gun, but there was no time now to seek one. The Gopher Kid had got the gate unlocked and was swinging it inward and preparing to lead his horse through. Rowdy wrenched the feathered sombrero from his own head and placed it upon Felicia's. "Up into saddles!" he urged, boosting her aboard his own horse and climbing aboard the borrowed one. "Do you think you can find that mountain tavern where I first saw you?"

She looked bewildered for a moment, then nodded her head. "It's that way, isn't it?" she asked, waving her hand in the right direction.

"We're rushing that gate," Rowdy said. "I'm going to try and fix it so that one of us makes it. If you get through, wait for me at Halfway House. And hang on to that feathered J. B. and those papers meanwhile! Do you savvy?"

She nodded. He smiled at her, remembering all the questions he'd wanted to ask and never had a chance. Who was she, and what had fetched her to the Bearclaw, and why was she a prisoner of this rancho? The questions would have to keep.

"You first!" he said and slapped hard at her horse. "The Kid will have a moment when he'll be too surprised to act."

Her horse bolted forward, heading toward the opened gate and through it, nearly riding the astonished Gopher Kid down. After her, at a hard gallop, came Rowdy Dow. But the Kid, veering aside as Felicia had swept by him, had now leaped into his saddle and was dragging at a gun — an instinctive gesture. He got the weapon out as Rowdy came roaring by, and the Kid swung the gun, the barrel clipping Rowdy alongside the head.

There was just a single moment of clarity when Rowdy thought to kick free of his stirrups and to wrap his arms around the Kid. Then the lights went out for Rowdy, but as he fell from his horse he was dragging the Kid with him, for he clung to the Kid with a woodtick's tenacity. Thus was Rowdy giving Felicia her chance, and his last hazy thought was a hope that she was getting away free.

CHAPTER XI

THE LONESOME LAMB

Stumpy Grampis sat forlornly upon a deadfall log in the afternoon sunshine, as frustrated as a boy who's just been told that the Fourth of July has been struck from the calendar. True to orders, he'd raised a mighty fuss, had Stumpy. He had heated up his shooting iron to the melting point, almost stripping his belt of cartridges, and the sum total of all this had been nothing. Absolutely nothing! Confound Rowdy Dow for a coin-flipping galoot who'd been lucky enough to corral all the fun for himself! Stumpy would have felt more useful if he were a wooden Indian in front of a cigar store. At least he'd be handy for drunks to lean against!

For Stumpy, in spite of the many protests he voiced as regarded a life of derring do, was a man who liked to be up to his hairy ears in the thick of things, and right now he was feeling as useless as a hole in a rain barrel. He'd carried out orders, dang it! It had been his not to reason why, his but to do or die, but the valley of death into which he'd valiantly ridden had been about as thrilling as a snort of sarsaparilla. A fine thing! A man stuck his neck out, just asking for it to be shot at, and nobody was considerate enough to oblige him!

"You and Stumpy wiggle your way through the woods," Rowdy had told him and Don Sebastian, "and get across the road to the ranch and move along the fence a mile or so to the west . . ." Well, by grab, they'd done just that. Keeping to the cover of the timber, they'd moved far south, then risked crossing the road. After that they'd turned northward and approached the fence to Rancho Del Diablo and skirted the fence to the west, still concealing themselves in the trees and scanning the guarded acres from cover. Don Sebastian had taken charge then.

"Ees a good place to raise the beeg fuss," the caballero had decided. "You weel go half a mile farther, senor, and starts the gons to banging, no?"

"I'm your huckleberry," Stumpy had said, giving his pants a hitch.

And so he had moved to this spot and started his fireworks, echoing the tumult Don Sebastian Gregorio Jose de Ibarra y Alvarez was making to the east. The object of this game had been, of course, to draw Trimble's vaqueros to this vicinity, thus giving Rowdy his chance to cut the fence at a distant point. But had the vaqueros showed up? Not in Stumpy's vicinity. He had perforated the sky with might and main, working at the chore with a zeal that would have won him a citation from any sensible general; and other guns had taken up the chorus. But whoever had been drawn to the fence had been drawn to the section where Don Sebastian was at work. You'd have thought Stumpy had some sort of plague! Confound it, they'd treated him like he was one of them fellers in a *leper* colony!

Still, he kept his gun a-going, and after some time the firing died to the east of him. Leaving the thicket of brush from which he'd operated, Stumpy ventured nearer the fence. His view was limited by a clump of trees beyond the barbed wire, but he thought he saw a sizeable group of riders heading away, deeper into the guarded domain. Whereupon Stumpy had seated himself upon the deadfall log and cursed a destiny that had deprived him of any real excitement. Don Sebastian would be gloating, confound him! But there was nothing left to do but go and be gloated at, so Stumpy at last sought his horse which he'd left tied to a stout bush, hauled himself into the saddle and turned toward the spot where he'd parted company with the caballero.

He found the place easily enough, and there was plenty of spent shells in the vicinity to testify that Don Sebastian had been no sluggard. But the Mexican himself was missing. Hide and hair, tooth and toenail. Stumpy unleashed his sulphuric vocabulary, and then the cold hand of fear clutched him with the thought that Don Sebastian might have stopped a bullet and crawled into the brush to die. "Pore jigger!" Stumpy murmured, suffused with contrition, but a hasty look-see revealed no fresh corpse. Stumpy peered toward the fence. Had the caballero been captured? But no, the fence was intact, and the gate was a mile or so to the east, which meant that those who'd been drawn to the fence had not come any closer.

Don Sebastian, then, had embarked upon an expedition of his own and left no forwarding address. A fine howdy-you-do! Stumpy told the trees a few things about Mexicans in general, and a certain caballero in particular, then hauled himself into his saddle again. He felt a little lost, a little lonesome, and so much at loose ends as to have no plan of procedure. He might try cutting sign on Don Sebastian, but the Mexican had proved himself a will-o'-the-wisp heretofore, and the effort would likely be futile. Better to head back to where they'd left Rowdy and see how the lie of the land looked there.

That meant crossing the road again, and Stumpy turned southward for a considerable distance, keeping to the timber, and it was late afternoon when he ventured upon the road. It was as empty as a rum barrel after a Siwash celebration, and since he was now a great distance below Rancho Del Diablo, he risked the road for a mile or so, then left it to water his horse from Bearclaw Creek. He was at this task when he heard the *clip-clop* of hoofs coming along the road, down out of the north. Stumpy drew his mount deeper into the willows embroidering the creek bank and stood with his hand clamped tightly over the horse's nostrils.

Big among the dozen riders who loped by was Abel Karst. The Shootin' Soreheads, then, were still prowling the vicinity, and for a moment Stumpy had an urge to call out to them. These men were sworn enemies of Rancho Del Diablo, and thus in a sense they had a common cause with Stumpy. But, remembering that cabin calaboose in Bear- claw, Stumpy decided against showing himself. Dang it, he was a man caught be-twixt and between!

Karst's crew disappearing to the south,

Stumpy returned to the road, crossed it, and skirted the slope northward, keeping again to the concealment of the timber. A fine way to travel this was! First thing he knew, two of his horse's legs would be shorter than the other two! It was nearly dark when he reached the spot were he and Don Sebastian had parted company with Rowdy; and Rowdy was nowhere about. Venturing down to the fence, Stumpy found where it had been cut. Rowdy, then, had succeeded in getting inside the guarded domain.

For a long time Stumpy tussled with a mighty temptation, his urge being to follow Rowdy into the ranch. Confound it, Rowdy was probably up to his ears in trouble right now and needed somebody with Stumpy's capabilities to extricate him! Stumpy was near to selling himself a solid bill of goods along this line when he remembered Rowdy saying, "If . . . we lose track of each other, we can meet at Halfway House . . ." Supposing Rowdy had gone into the ranch and come out again and was already on his way to a rendezvous at the mountain tavern? A fine howdy-you-do if Stumpy tangled the twine by heading into the ranch while Rowdy was elsewhere.

Stumpy sighed a calliope-like sigh. Truly a man was beset with the making of many decisions. Tugging at his down-tilted moustache, Stumpy recalled a bit of advice his dear, departed father had given him long ago. "Gabriel, if you are ever tempted to think for yourself," his father had said, "don't!" The fact that the old man had been in jail at the time, caught trying to pass a three-dollar bill of his own manufacture, lessened not one with the sagacity of his advice. Sighing again, Stumpy decided to hew to the line and head for Halfway House as per the original arrangement.

All of which necessitated another decision. There were two ways to get to the mountain tavern. He could head south, almost to Bearclaw, then cross below the ridge and head northward, following the trail he and Rowdy had taken at a high lope when they'd fled from Karst's crew the night before. That was the long way. The other choice was to climb the ridge again and drop down the other side. That was the hard way. But somewhere south, Stumpy remembered, were the Shootin' Soreheads. He looked upward at the ridge, scowled, and began the ascent.

Dang it all! Fate had shuffled him a fistful of deuces for sure!

The darkness came quickly. He was soon leading his horse and floundering up a slippery trail, and he grew increasingly mindful that he was both hungry and weary. He lost his way, careened into bushes and trees and invented new swear words which astonished even himself. The moon rose, but it gave no more light than you'd get from an anæmic firefly; and by the time Stumpy had finally topped the ridge, he was too exhausted to contemplate making the descent this night. Hobbling his horse, he spread his saddle blanket, rolled himself into it and tried to sleep. But it was cold enough up here to give a brass monkey a bad case of pneumonia, and sleep refused to come.

"I'm just a pore lost, lonesome lamb," he told himself, wanting the company of his own voice. "I've been forgot by the sheepherder, and I'm out in the blizzard with not enough wool on me to keep a flea warm. I'm likely to freeze my pore little tail right down to the nub, but there ain't nobody givin' a hoot. No, sir, nobody cares about a pore lost little lonesome lamb adrift in a cold, cruel world . . ."

To this saturnalia of self-pity, he finally dozed off and awakened to the dawn light to stir himself from the blanket. Remembering there was food to be had at Halfway House, he began the descent of the slope with enthusiasm, and before noon he was nearing the mountain tavern. Mindful that the Shootin' Soreheads seemed to have a way of being everywhere at once, he approached cautiously, but when he ventured into the clearing, the huge, two-storied log structure had an air of utter desertion.

Stumpy went first to the stable, hoping against hope that he'd find Rowdy's horse there, and so convinced was he that he wouldn't that when he saw the mount he whooped with joy. Slapping his own horse into a stall, he went bow-legging to the main building, mounted the gallery and climbed through the ravaged window. "Rowdy, old hoss!" he shouted. "It's me! Your partner! If you was a girl, I'd kiss you!"

Then Stumpy was staring in surprise, for she *was* a girl — a dark-haired, beautiful girl in riding breeches and an embroidered jacket, a girl who'd been sitting at one of the tables, her head resting upon her folded arms, sleeping. Stumpy's wild entry had brought her awake, and she looked up with startled eyes; and Stumpy, speechless for a moment, finally found his tongue. "Where's Rowdy?" he demanded.

"Rowdy?"

"My partner. His hoss is out in the stable."

"Ah," she said, "the brave gringo who

came to my rescue in Rancho Del Diablo. His name I never knew. Alas, senor, I fear he was captured after enabling me to escape."

"Say!" Stumpy ejaculated, understanding beginning to percolate within him. "You're Felicia, the gal who waved to Rowdy from a window of this shebang. Doggone it, I was always of a mind that Rowdy only dreamed you. Even after he showed me what you wrote in the dust of the window sill."

She said, "And I remember you now, senor. You are the little man who was with this Senor Rowdy that stormy night. You are his partner, you say?"

"Wa-al, I'm more like a father to him," Stumpy said with a great show of modesty. "Sort of combination of advisor and protector, you might say. Rowdy's a galoot with a knack for getting into trouble. Me, I sort of tag along to get him out." He frowned, dragged from fancy to fact. "You say he was captured?"

She told him of Rowdy's entry into her bedroom the night before and of the incident at the gate when one had escaped and one had stayed behind. "He gave me his horse," she said in conclusion. "He knew it was fast. He told me to meet him here. I got to the fence and found it was still cut.

I wasn't sure of directions, but I felt that this place was on this side of the slope. All night I climbed through timber, first up, then down. I have just recently arrived here, senor, and I am very weary."

Stumpy had spied the feathered sombrero which she had placed upon the bar. "You said Rowdy gave you the hat?"

"Also some documents," she said, indicating the front of her blouse. "I am to keep them until he is able to join me."

Stumpy frowned. Like Rowdy, he had many questions he wanted to ask this girl, but, also like Rowdy, he conceded that this was neither the time nor the place. "I'm going out to the stable to fork down some hay for my horse," he said. "Then I'm getting outside some grub. After that I'm taking the trail back to Rancho Del Diablo. Doggone it, I knew danged well I should have headed into that spread when I was at the hole in the fence! Rowdy's likely needing me mighty bad."

He stepped back out through the window; Felicia followed him. "If you go, I shall go with you, senor," she said as they strode toward the stable. "It is my fault that this Senor Rowdy is now in peril."

"Now look," Stumpy said darkly. "I ain't one for being cluttered up with female wimmin." Into the stable, he climbed to the loft and found a pitchfork and ladled hay down into a manger below. When he descended, he said, "We'll argue it out as we eat. My stummick feels like it's been left on the doorstep of an empty house."

Again they crawled through the broken window, Stumpy gallantly giving his hand to the lady. Then he cast his eyes about the place, wondering where the dead proprietor kept his food stock. And, taking this look, Stumpy's jaw unhinged and nearly dragged to his knees, and he raised a quivering finger and pointed. "This dang shebang is cursed!" he squawked. "Look!"

"What is it, senor?" Felicia demanded, bewilderment in her eyes.

"That feathered J. B.!" Stumpy ejaculated. "It was there on the bar when we went out to the barn. Now it's gone. Disappeared. Turned into smoke. Lady, this here establishment is just about as wrong as two left feet!"

CHAPTER XII

COLT CASTANETS

Rowdy had the sensation of swimming in a whirlpool of ink with an anvil around his neck. Clawing upward, he came back to consciousness to find lamplight hammering at his eyelids; and when he opened his eyes he saw scowling faces. One belonged to Gideon Turk; the other to the Gopher Kid. Rowdy scowled, too, and rolled over on his side, determined to dredge up a better dream than the one he seemed to be having. Then memory came back to him — the memory of the encounter with the Kid at the gate, and the blow that had brought oblivion. Rowdy groaned. This was no dream.

"He isn't dead," Turk said in a low, ominous voice. "Not yet."

Rowdy's head felt as though eighteen prospectors were inside, all of them diligently plying picks in an effort to uncover pay dirt. Glancing around, he found himself on a low divan in that big main room of the hacienda. Only two people seemed to be with him — Turk, fully dressed, lean and cadaverous and looking ten feet tall as he loomed over Rowdy; the diminutive Gopher Kid looking a little crumpled around the edges, looking angry.

Felicia? Rowdy wanted to ask about her, wanted to know if she'd made her getaway, but he had a strong hunch he was here only to answer questions, not to ask them; he had a hunch that that was why he was being kept alive. The Gopher Kid, his close-set eyes colder than ever, drew a gun and took a lunging step toward the divan, raising the gun.

"Put that down, you fool!" Turk barked.

Turk's glance fixed Rowdy with almost hypnotic intensity. "You look alive enough to talk!" he snapped. "Now you're going to tell me what fetched you here."

Rowdy grinned weakly. "Why, you did, Captain. Don't you remember the advt. in the Miles City paper?"

"I'm through with bluffing," Turk said. "Buck Trimble is dead!"

"Should I swoon with surprise?" Rowdy's grin broadened. "I had a look into a window of the wing. I saw his body. That was before I tangled my twine the first time. But you wanted to play Captain Trimble, Turk, so I thought I'd humour you. You'd better get the captain underground, amigo, if you want to put on a good show of passing yourself off as him."

"Captain Trimble will be buried as soon as a fancy coffin I've ordered for him has arrived," Turk said. "Fortunately, one of my men knows the art of embalming."

"Enough to patch up the bullet hole you probably put in Trimble?"

"Buck Trimble died from natural causes. You seem to have guessed my identity, Dow. What you don't seem to realise is that I'm master here. For years I was Captain Trimble's right hand, the man who enabled him to build this empire. Now that he's dead, I'm his sole heir and can prove it by a will that will stand in any court. But this evasive talk will get you nowhere, Dow. I want to know what really fetched you here!"

Rowdy swung his legs to the floor and got into a sitting position, an effort that made his head spin. He was not tied, but neither was he armed; and the Gopher Kid instantly took another step nearer, his hand again swooping to the gun he'd cased.

"You'd better talk!" the Kid said savagely.

"Oh, yes. You want to know what fetched me. Well, to start with, it was that notice in the Miles City paper. After that, I thought I'd go into the button-collecting business, Turk. I picked one up in Halfway House a couple of nights ago — tore it off a galoot who dragged Felicia away in the darkness. When you showed up in Bearclaw the next morning, I couldn't help but notice you had a button missing from your coat. It's still missing."

Gideon Turk glanced down at his coat, surprise making him ludicrous for a moment. Then: "So you knew I was just posing at the time?"

"Maybe," Rowdy said. "We might as well face the cards. Buck Trimble had a job for me to do, so he put that notice in the paper. Naturally that was before he died. But when he did pass on, which must have been recently, you knew I was heading this way looking for him. My guess is that you didn't want me snooping around Rancho Del Diablo, so you schemed to meet me in Bearclaw and pass yourself off as the captain. Right so far?"

"Go on, Dow."

"Since a job had been promised me, I was likely to be suspicious if you showed up and claimed there wasn't any job. So you spun a windy about wanting a sword out of a Mexico City museum. Maybe there is such a sword, but you don't want it any more than you want the Big Dipper down out of the sky. But if you could have talked me into taking that pasear, you'd have got me plumb out of the country. It was a good idea, only it didn't work. I wasn't buying any trips to *Mejico*. But you were satisfied just the same. You figured I'd be leaving the Bearclaw country pronto, thinking I'd come on a wild goose chase."

Turk smiled a cold smile. "And what other deductions have you made, Mr. Dow?"

Rowdy waved a hand airily. His head was not throbbing as much; he wondered if he could walk if he made the try but decided against it.

"I've jumped to the notion that this buck-toothed little killer is in on whatever you're up to. That's why, when he captured Stumpy and me out at the fence gate this morning he decided to string us up as soon as he heard our names. His method of getting rid of us was a little more direct than the scheme you were trying to pull off in Bearclaw, Turk. And his method might have fixed us up for good, only we didn't swing. So to-night you tried drugging me. You figured you could grab a little peaceful sleep, and when the Kid got back you'd have him finish me off. That chore would be more in his line."

"You gave the brandy to Pedro Montez!" Turk exclaimed in sudden understanding.

"I found him fast asleep when the guns at the gate aroused me. But he wasn't asleep when I first went to bed."

"The drug hadn't had time to work then," Rowdy admitted.

"You meddling fool!" Turk blazed. "What will it take to convince you that Rancho Del Diablo is bad medicine for you?"

"A girl needed help," Rowdy said calmly. "You see, Turk, she managed to leave a message at Halfway House the other night. You didn't know that, eh? And there was the real Buck Trimble who had a proposition for me. I hadn't guessed he was dead, so I came here tonight. You still wanted to play Buck Trimble, so I strung along. Now I know I had you worried and you wanted the answers to some questions before you put the Injin sign on me. You had to know what had brought me here, but I got you to believe I'd changed my mind about that Mexico pasear."

Only one lamp burned in this room; it sat upon a table not far from the divan, and the light bothered Rowdy's eyes. Instinctively he reached to move the lamp, and instantly the Gopher Kid's gun appeared. "Keep yore hands to yoreself!" the Kid snapped.

Turk said, "So you were running a bluff to-night, Dow!"

"Both of us, Turk. Weren't we the cute little pair, though!"

A mighty anger shook Gideon Turk. "Well, you succeeded in getting Felicia away from here. She made her escape, thanks to your holding on to the Kid. But some of my riders are out now, and the rest will be combing the range fine come morning. You've made a very great nuisance of yourself, but you're going to answer a couple more questions before I start squaring up for that!"

Elation leaped into Rowdy's eyes. This was his first inkling that Felicia had indeed escaped; she might, he supposed, have been a prisoner elsewhere in this hacienda right now. He wondered how long he'd lain unconscious and judged that it probably hadn't been for more than an hour. He looked towards the doors; they seemed a million miles away. The nearest window was much closer at hand, and its iron grillwork was open, but the Gopher Kid saw Rowdy's quick stare, and the Kid instinctively moved himself to be in a position to block any rush toward the window.

"What else is troubling you, Mr. Turk?" Rowdy asked.

"The feathered sombrero," Turk said. "You must have come into my room and taken it before you got out of the hacienda. Was that your idea or the girl's?"

"I think I'll keep you guessing," Rowdy said.

But Gideon Turk didn't seem to hear him, for Turk was deep in thought, and then, suddenly, he snapped his bony fingers. *"The sombrero!"* he said breathlessly. "Kid, we never thought of that! I was hanging tight to that hat since it represented the kind of authority the vaqueros understood. But the feathered sombrero is the answer to *everything!* And now it's gone!"

He glared at Rowdy. "You gave it to the girl, didn't you? Why, Dow? What is it you know?"

Rowdy shook his head. "Supposing I told you there just isn't any answer to that one?"

"You mean you won't talk?"

"I mean that the J. B. meant nothing to me. I picked it up for a man who wanted it. No, I'm not going to tell you his name. You'd have your riders hunting him down, and he's twice proved himself a friend of mine."

"That damn' greaser!" Turk ejaculated. "Don Sebastian, he calls himself! Am I right, Dow?"

Rowdy shrugged. "Let's say you're warm. You seem to know all about Don Sebastian.

My guess is that you're the one who laid him out on the trail near Halfway House the other night."

Turk glanced at the Gopher Kid. "I guess we know everything now that we need to know," Turk said. "This man is just a meddler with a flair for gallantry. It was mostly the girl who fetched him here, I'm thinking. The other damage he did was just by chance. But he did it, most thoroughly. We've got to get into saddles. We've got to get that feathered sombrero back!"

The Kid's hysterical giggle rose. "But first — ?" he said eagerly.

"First we've got to make sure there'll be no further meddling from Mr. Rowdy Dow!"

"Let me have him," the Kid said, giggling again. "I know lots of ways. Slow ways."

"Be damned to slow ways!" Turk snapped. "We haven't time, and this man has proved too slippery before. I want him taken care of fast, and I want to be sure the job's through. Right here and now is the time and place!"

The Gopher Kid drew his gun again and stepped back a pace or two, a great delight in his little eyes. And Rowdy, watching him, turned cold inside and tensed himself, placing the heels of his hands against the divan and preparing to leap. It would be suicide to jump the Kid, but at least there'd be the satisfaction of going out fighting. He saw the Kid's gun lift and level, and then the room was echoing gun-thunder. But it wasn't the Kid who'd fired. Not the first shot. Flame had leaped from the direction of the open window, and the Kid swerved sideways, fright in his face. His gun exploded, but the bullet only jarred a picture on the far wall. Someone was serenading at the window, using Colt castanets. The unseen gun spoke again, and the lamp blotted out.

Rowdy instantly dived for the floor and scuttled crabfashion toward the window. A friend was out there — Stumpy Grampis, Rowdy judged in the first frenzied moment. The Gopher Kid was firing again, angrily, blindly, the flame lighting up the room intermittently, the smell of powder growing heavy in the air. But Rowdy had reached the window; he folded his arms over his head and dived through, landing in a heap on the ground outside. Someone tugged at his arm, helping him to his feet.

"Stumpy — ?" Rowdy queried.

"No, eet is I, senor. Don Sebastian Gregorio Jose —"

"Never mind the rest of it!" Rowdy advised. "Let's get out of here!"

They were to the front of the building, and they began running within the enclosure between the building and the high adobe wall, but they had covered only a dozen yards when Don Sebastian tugged at Rowdy's elbow. "Here, senor!" the caballero hissed. "Over the wall!"

He made a stirrup of his hands, and Rowdy stepped upward, grasped the top of the wall and pulled himself to a prone position. Extending his hand to Don Sebastian, he gave a mighty heave and the Mexican scrambled to a perch beside him. Almost directly below them stood Don Sebastian's horse with the silver-encrusted saddle, anchored by trailing reins. The two dropped to the ground on the far side of the wall, and the caballero vaulted to the saddle, Rowdy climbing up behind him.

"I am leest-ning at the window before I shoot," said Don Sebastian. "Eet is true that Felicia is escape? And the feathered sombrero is weeth her, no? Then the work here is finish', and we do — how you say? — stir the dost!"

"Stir the dust!" Rowdy agreed. Already he could hear an uproar on the far side of the wall, voices calling, voices answering, the stampeding of booted feet and bare feet on the tiling. "And we're riding double!" Rowdy groaned. "They'll head us off in a hurry."

Don Sebastian, feeding his silver spurs to the mount, chuckled. "I am have the look aroun' before I find the window where I see you," he said. "While I am looking, I find the stable. I make one beeg bridle out of all the bridles, and then I lace the stirrups of all the saddles together. Was *mucho* fon. It weel take some time, senor, before the vaqueros are riding."

"Good for you!" Rowdy exclaimed. "And I'm mighty glad to see you. You came through the break in the fence?"

"Many hours ago. I am hiding in the trees for a long time, senor, waiting to get near thees place. I make the bargain with you to raise the foss and let you cut the fence. But I do not promise not to come into Rancho Del Diablo myself. But ees no need. You have done the work for me."

"Where's Stumpy?"

Don Sebastian shrugged. "When we part to raise the foss, I do not wait for him after. He is one brave caballero, that Senor Stumpy, but is no reason why he should share the reesks any further, no?"

Rowdy chuckled. "I'll bet Stumpy won't thank you for your attitude. Likely he's gone to Halfway House. I sent the senorita there, too."

They were beelining straight overland in the direction of the hole in the fence, and Rowdy, looking behind him until a rise of land hid the hacienda from view, saw no sign of pursuit. He was stricken for a moment with the remembrance that Gideon Turk, earlier that night, had given a vaquero orders for the mending of the fence, but, since Felicia seemed to have made good her escape, Rowdy judged that the wire hadn't been repaired. Yet riders must be abroad; the fence, he'd been told, was patrolled night and day.

They saw none of the vaqueros as they galloped along, and Rowdy was beginning to think that the vigilance of Rancho Del Diablo was vastly overrated. Then a thought struck him. Quetzalcoatl! The Aztec god had appeared to the vaqueros to-day, and the memory of him was probably all too fresh. Rancho Del Diablo's riders were likely huddled somewhere in superstitious dread when they should have been about their duties. Once again Rowdy was grateful to Quetzalcoatl.

He was even more grateful when they at last reached the fence and found the wire still cut at the spot where Rowdy had made his entry. And no riders were nearby to challenge their exit. They got through the fence and headed into the timber of the slope beyond it, and soon they had to dismount and begin toiling upward afoot.

Somewhere ahead of them to-night, doubtless, was Felicia — Felicia with the feathered sombrero and the document Captain Trimble had left for Rowdy. Somewhere ahead, then, might be all the answers to all the questions.

CHAPTER XIII

SECRET OF THE SOMBRERO

They came humping up the ridge in the last of the darkness, reaching the crest just as the dawn set the eastern hills afire, and thus, if Rowdy and Don Sebastian had only known it, they were not far behind Stumpy as they began the descent. They were tired and hungry and dishevelled, and Rowdy's head still ached, and he had the feeling of having been dragged through a knot hole six sizes too small, but elation gave him impetus on the last long miles. He had dared the dangers of Rancho Del Diablo and come through with his hide reasonably intact, and that was something to shout about.

Not that the danger was passed. Not by a jugful. That feathered sombrero had some special significance, and Gideon Turk had only last night become aware of it. Turk and his savage riders, along with the kill-crazy Gopher Kid, would be scouring the landscape to-day. And there was Abel Karst with his Shootin' Soreheads to dodge. Truly, the woods would be a-stir from here on out. But Rowdy was free as the unfettered zephyrs at the moment, and food and shelter and friends were ahead.

They came into the clearing before Halfway House in mid-morning; and someone was stirring in the stable. They dismounted and approached afoot, Don Sebastian with a gun in his hand; but it was Stumpy and Felicia who emerged to meet them, leading saddled horses. All concerned had a look, and Stumpy chortled, "Rowdy, old hoss! I was just on my way to rescue yuh!" Then Stumpy's face fell with the realisation that destiny had just fetched him another kick in the pants. "You might 'a' waited," he added in an aggrieved voice.

"Don Sebastian turned the trick," said Rowdy. "We owe him another favour. Alvarez, you're entitled to an extra clout over the head. But introductions are in order. Or do you know Felicia?"

Don Sebastian had already swept his sombrero away and was bending in a bow that almost scraped his forehead against the ground. "Ah, senorita," he said fervently, "please pardon the poor bungler who failed you in the hour of need. My face eet is *escarlata,* Senorita Quintera."

"Quintera — ?" Rowdy echoed, starting.

The girl took a step toward Don Sebastian, her eyes softening. "No apology is necessary, Senor Alvarez," she said. "I see that your head is bandaged. Doubtless you receive your wound in my service. It is I who should be humble at this moment."

"The leetle dove is no more gracious than you, senorita," said Don Sebastian. "The wild rose, growing in the theeckets in old *Mejico* is not half so beautiful as you. The sun, he is hide his face, knowing he is outshone when he is gazing upon you. The graceful gazelle, bounding upon the heeltops is —"

"Hey!" said Rowdy. "I'm still here!"

Felicia crossed to him and took his hand. "And I am indebted to you, senor, and happy to see you alive."

"It was nothing," Rowdy said. "When I first saw you here a couple of nights ago, I said to myself, now there's a girl who needs a friend. Anything I can do to help her will be appreciated. I could see it in your face. Like a white shadow it was, pressed there against the window. Or like a flower —"

"Gawd!" Stumpy wailed. "It's bit you, too, Rowdy! Am I the only jigger in the whole dang world who ain't gone loco?"

"Humpf!" said Rowdy. "Is there anything to eat in yonder shebang?"

Felicia plucked at his sleeve. "I have sorry news," she said dolefully. "After all you did for me, I failed you. I brought the feathered sombrero here, as you asked, senor, but it disappeared not long ago. Please don't think I was completely careless. I looked through the building when I first arrived, and I will swear no one was here."

Rowdy was far too used to the mysteries of Halfway House to be stunned by such news, and it was Don Sebastian who took on a pained expression. "You've still got those papers, senorita?" Rowdy asked.

Wordlessly she took the two envelopes from her blouse and passed them to Rowdy.

"Somebody must 'a' sneaked through the window and lifted the hat while me and the senorita was out in the stable," Stumpy said. "Ain't nothin' can be done about it. I found some canned goods. We just et before we saddled up. Come along and I'll fix you and Don Sebastian some grub."

The three horses put in the stable, they walked toward the mountain tavern. Inside, Stumpy fell to preparing food, and Rowdy, seated at a table along with Don Sebastian and Felicia said, "We've all proved ourselves friends. I think it's time some cards were faced."

"Ees good idea, senor," Don Sebastian agreed.

Whereupon Rowdy told what had fetched

him and his partner to the Bearclaw country, sparing none of the details; and when he'd finished he looked at Don Sebastian, expecting a like confidence. But the caballero, his eyes glued on Felicia's face, appeared not to have been listening. Sighing, Rowdy ran his thumb under the flap of the envelope he had got from the book in Buck Trimble's library.

"I'll read this aloud," he said. Stumpy placed food before him, and Rowdy forked up a few mouthfuls, then shook out the flimsy sheets of the letter, instantly recognising the same broad, sprawling fist that had adorned the note the Bearclaw hotel clerk had given him.

"There seems to be quite a lot of it," Rowdy observed and brought the pages closer to his eyes. "This, in a sense," he read, "is the confession of a man who has come to realise in the lateness of his years that his life has been misspent. To those who have felt the weight of my heel, I make this apology and this attempt at restitution. Perhaps it is not yet too late . . ."

"He doesn't sound like such a bad jigger," Stumpy observed.

Rowdy had another bite to eat. Then: "My life has been a violent one, dedicated to grasping for power. Now, in my twilight,

I've come to realise the futility of such an ambition as I possessed. I have also come to realise that I have been in a sense the tool of a man whose craftiness matched my own blind ruthlessness. That man is Gideon Turk . . ."

"Ees one bad hombre, Senor Turk," Don Sebastian agreed.

Rowdy turned a page. "Few men are ever granted the privilege of seeing themselves as others see them, but that dubious pleasure became mine in a queer way and was the turning point of my life. In San Francisco a few years ago I chanced into a waxwork museum where were depicted various nefarious characters. And there, side by side with such rogues as Billy the Kid, Jesse James, Geronomo, the Apache, I saw myself standing. The reputation I had carved had made me eligible, even in my own lifetime, for inclusion. It gave me a great deal of food for thought. It gave me pause to reflect upon the life I'd led and to consider amends . . ."

Felicia said in astonishment, "He was a good man — a good man after all . . ."

"My early life will be of no interest to those this document will affect except that I might say that a career as a professional revolutionist and soldier of fortune instilled in me certain characteristics which I've since come to deplore. My original ranch was forged in my middle years and overlapped the border. My claim to it was made legal by a man I had befriended, a certain Gideon Turk, lawyer by profession and rogue by nature. Through his machinations we managed to seize acreage that was the property of Don Carlos Quintera whose family had controlled the land for generations under an old Spanish land grant. Turk found the loophole in the Quintera claim, and they were evicted. But Don Carlos was a fighter, and until the time of his death he plagued me with so much trouble that I decided to move my herds northwards to new graze . . ."

Rowdy glanced at Felicia. "Now you can see why I jumped when I learned your full name just this morning," he said. "I knew that Trimble's original ranch was carved out in part from the old Quintera land grant."

"Read on, please, senor!" Felicia urged.

"In Montana a new ranch was established. Again Gideon Turk's faculty for finding legal loopholes played a part. We ousted a number of landholders whose names I have appended to this document. Like Don Carlos, they have continued to fight me and to curse my name . . ."

"The Shootin' Soreheads!" Stumpy ejaculated.

"My will," Rowdy continued, "prepared a number of years ago, made Gideon Turk my sole heir and is in his possession. After my trip to San Francisco and my change of heart, I told him I planned to make restitution to those I'd robbed, even though the robbery had been sanctioned in the eyes of the law. He scoffed at first, then grew belligerent. I then secretly prepared a new will, one which returns a great part of my Montana holdings to Abel Karst and the others from whom they were wrested. The rest of my land, the cattle and buildings are to go to the only living descendant of Don Carlos Quintera, his granddaughter Felicia . . ."

The girl began crying softly, and Rowdy hastily resumed his reading.

"Of late I have realised that my life is in danger. I made the mistake of telling Gideon Turk of my new will, and I have reason to believe he has been scheming against me with a man known as the Gopher Kid who was hired as foreman at Turk's insistence. I have placed much of this information with the Mexican government, asking them to locate Felicia Quintera for me, and since then I have advertised in several papers in an effort to enlist the aid of a certain Rowdy

Dow who seems qualified to assist me in the restitution I have in mind. Turk knows of this, also, and my fear is that he will find the means to kill me before the arrival of Dow. If this should reach Dow's hands, as I hope and plan that it shall, I hereby commission him to see that my will is placed in Felicia Quintera's possession and to assist her in making the proper restitution to Karst and his followers. I also commission Dow, in the event of my death, to determine the nature of my death and to bring my murderer to justice. For these services, Dow is to receive ten thousand dollars from my estate . . ."

"And where's the danged will?" Stumpy demanded.

"I have for a number of years," Rowdy read, "been the possessor of a queer feathered sombrero which I had fashioned in Mexico to suit a whim of mine. My second will has been sewed into the lining of this feathered sombrero . . ."

Don Sebastian spread his hands. "Now you see why I weesh to get the sombrero and why my face fall when I learn eet is gone."

"I'm beginning to see a lot," Rowdy said, laying down the flimsy document. "Gideon Turk had two worries — one to get rid of me, the other to lay his hands on Trimble's second will and destroy it. But it was only last night that he realised he'd been packing that new will inside the sombrero all along and never knew it. When the sombrero started interesting outsiders, Turk saw the light. Now he'll be hot-footing it after us for sure."

"Senor Turk had another worry," Felicia said. "Me. I have been living in El Paso for many years. Recently I received a letter from Senor Turk saying his employer, Senor Trimble, was deathly ill and wished to see me. Senor Turk requested that I come to this place, this Halfway House, and be here on a certain date, just a couple of days past. The Mexican government had already located me and informed me that Senor Trimble wished to make partial restitution for the wrong he'd done my family, but still I was suspicious — a Quintera had no reason to trust Captain Trimble. But I made the trip."

"And Turk came here looking for you that stormy night," Rowdy said.

Felicia nodded. "He made crazy talk, asking me to marry him and growing very angry when I refused. Then he urged me to come with him to Rancho Del Diablo and talk to Captain Trimble. I asked him to step from the room while I changed to clothes suitable for such weather. It was while he was in the hall that I tried in my desperation to signal you, Senor Dow, seeing you in the yard, and, failing that, I traced a message in the dust on the window sill."

"But Turk got suspicious," Rowdy guessed, "and dragged you from the room, clouting me down when I got in his way. I see his notion. He wanted his hands on Buck Trimble's heir, and the marriage idea was so he'd be master of the ranch even if the second will did show up. If he couldn't persuade you to marry him, he would have had to kill you."

His glance shuttled to Don Sebastian. "You're the one county we haven't heard from."

"I, senor," said Don Sebastian with a dramatic flourish, "am the Mexican government!"

"All of it?" Stumpy gasped.

"Oh, no, senor. Ees several other hombres besides myself. The information wheech Captain Treemble sent to Mexico City, eet is turn' over to me. I go to El Paso to find the Senorita Quintera. Such beauty I am finding! Such grace! Like the leetle gazelle —"

"Sure, sure," said Rowdy. "And you came here with her?"

"I am — how you say eet? — tagging along after I have tell her she is Treemble's heir. But the other night on the trail I am a leetle bit lost, so I stake out my horse and climb a tree for look. When I am come down, I meet thees Senor Turk and tell heem that I, Don Sebastian, seek a place called Halfway House to meet a beautiful senorita. Bang! The lights go out!"

"Turk knew your name last night," Rowdy mused. "He learned it from you, of course."

"When I am wake up, I am here, senors, and you are caring for me. I remember your face from the reward posters, Senor Dow, but I don't know that you are working for Senor Treemble. After you go, I hear the beeg fight in the hall and I leave to chase thees Senor Turk who is carrying away the beautiful Felicia. Ees no good; he has got sweeft horse and I, *ay de mi,* have none. When I get the horse and try to get inside Rancho Del Diablo, I am almost shot full of holes. Then I find you, senors, and make the bargain."

"Now we all know where we stand," Rowdy said. "But the heck of it is that we need the feathered sombrero, and it's gone." He began drumming his fingertips on the table. "Maybe there *was* somebody hiding in here, senorita, and you didn't look close enough. Remember the jigger, Stumpy, who had a lamp burning when we rode up with Karst chasing us? When you and Felicia went to the stable this morning, he could have grabbed the hat."

"I theenk," Don Sebastian said darkly, "we make a good search of thees beel-ding."

"That's a notion," Rowdy agreed.

They went together, the four of them, examining each of the upstairs rooms minutely and finding nothing to arouse their interest. They came back to the big bar-room and had a careful look, and Stumpy said, "What about the cellar, Rowdy?"

"We had a look there once," Rowdy said. "But we can look again." Heading behind the bar, he hoisted the trap-door and groped down the steps to the dark, stone-walled, dirt-floored little room. Scraping a match aglow, he'd just about decided that nothing had changed when something caught his eye. He picked up the articles that had aroused his interest and brought them back to the bar-room.

"Take a look," he said.

He was holding a false beard, black and bushy and rigged to be hooked over a man's ears. Along with the beard he held up a black robe bordered with white crosses.

"The garb of Quetzalcoatl," he said. "Now we know where that Aztec god has been hiding when he hasn't been busy scaring the wits out of the vaqueros. And now we know who ran off with the feathered sombrero. Quetzalcoatl seems to have earthly interests. But how do we catch up with him?"

They were all staring in surprise — surprise and hopelessness — but Stumpy brightened. "Remember the village idiot who found the lost dog, Rowdy? They asked him how he did, and he said he just sat down and asked himself where he'd be if he was a dog, and he went there and there was the dog. All we got to do is figger the same way. If we was an Aztec god, where would we be?"

"Somewhere else," Rowdy said glumly.

Don Sebastian, stationed near the broken front window stirred with a new interest. "Ees company coming," he announced. "Senor Turk and his vaqueros. Eet looks like we shall have to make one beeg fight to defend a sombrero which we don' got!"

CHAPTER XIV

AZTECS EVERYWHERE

Trouble, Rowdy reflected, was certainly a cumulative commodity. Trouble really gathered dividends. Take a good, round silver dollar and put it out as an investment, and what did you get? Rowdy's knowledge of banking was rather dim, having been largely garnered in his outlaw years when he'd done business with such institutions with a loaded gun and a ready tow-sack, yet he knew it took considerable time to double a dollar by orthodox means. But trouble doubled fast. Trouble didn't fool around.

Take the incident of Rowdy's answering the advertisement Captain Trimble had put in the paper. There was trouble for you, but hardly enough to be visible to the naked eye. But it had supplied the partners with chips in a game, and they'd really parleyed from such a start. Don Sebastian lying wounded on a mountain trail — gunfire in Halfway House — the cabin calaboose of the Shootin' Soreheads — flight in the night, and ropes around their necks under a cottonwood — Rancho Del Diablo and another wild flight — these were the chips they'd raked in. And now a ton of trouble had landed squarely upon their doorstep, for Turk and his vaqueros had caught up with them, and there was bound to be a fight.

Yet it was not surprising that Turk was hard on their heels. Turk had guessed the secret of the feathered sombrero last night, and Turk had intended then to cut sign on Felicia who'd escaped with the sombrero. When Rowdy had slipped through Turk's fingers, too, Turk had doubtless spent the rest of the dark hours in the saddle. Those Indian followers of his could probably smell out sign, even if it led through a stockyard, and thus Turk had trailed the fugitives to Halfway House. Rowdy had expected this to happen and had intended taking his friends and making himself scarce; but he'd tarried here too long. But the real irony of the situation had been expressed by Don Sebastian. Rowdy's crew would have to fight to protect a sombrero which they didn't have!

Rowdy, weaponless since leaving Rancho Del Diablo, had spied a six-shooter and belt behind the bar in his recent search, and he hurried now and got these articles. Crowding to the window beside the caballero, he saw a horde of horsemen in the clearing, and he had no trouble identifying black-clad Turk and the diminutive Gopher Kid among the vaqueros. The group was dismounting and Rowdy, tilting his gun, geysered dust in warning. "Here's where we start a war," Rowdy announced, watching in grim satisfaction as the vaqueros broke, bolting to the timber at the far side of the clearing.

For war it would have to be. No point in trying to parley, to explain to Turk that the sombrero was missing. Turk wouldn't believe them, and even if he did, he'd still push an attack. He'd wanted Rowdy dead last night, and he'd still be of the same mind. And Turk would either want Felicia dead or his prisoner again. Felicia was the real heir to Rancho Del Diablo and therefore the real threat to Turk's scheme of possession. Stumpy and Don Sebastian might not count much one way or another as far as Turk was concerned, they'd doomed themselves by virtue of being friends of Rowdy and Felicia.

Stumpy was at the window, too, and from the timber a volley poured, the bullets thunking into the log walls of the tavern, the voice of Gideon Turk shouting orders, the voice of the Gopher Kid rising in hysterical fury. There was a scurrying in the timber, the elusive movement of soft-footed men; and Stumpy said, "They're circling to surround the place. Rowdy, you figger a dose of skyrockets would bother 'em?"

Rowdy shook his head. "That worked the other night because it was dark and Karst's crew was bunched together. Not a chance now."

But at least they were in a good position to withstand a siege. There were only four windows to defend on the ground floor — two to the front of the building, two in the west wall. The bar ran along the east wall with no windows behind it. Glass fell from the two windows facing west, and by this token the besieged suddenly realised that some of the vaqueros had manœuvred around to attack that side of the building. Moving quickly, Don Sebastian and Stumpy went to guard those windows, squatting down beside them and exposing themselves intermittently to scatter lead, keeping the attackers at a distance. Rowdy found Felicia at his elbow, an ivory-handled six-shooter in her hand. Rowdy recognised the gun as a twin to the one Don Sebastian was using.

"You take the other front window, senor," Felicia said. "I will hold this one."

Rowdy was about to argue, to press the point that Felicia had better get behind the shelter of the bar; but something in her eyes bridled his tongue. She was the daughter of Don Carlos Quintera, and that meant she was of fighting stock.

Rowdy moved to the other front window. Smoke puffed from the timber, bullets hammering into the log walls, some finding their way through the windows to play havoc inside the big room. A bottle splintered on a shelf behind the bar, whisky gushing from the ruin; and Stumpy cursed wildly.

"Blast the uncivilised sons!" he shouted. "Ain't nothin' sacred to 'em?" Rearing upward at considerable risk, he fired rapidly, then bobbed to shelter.

The back door, heavily barred, would doubtless withstand artillery. But now that door was rattling to the impact of bullets, which proved that vaqueros were to the rear of the building, too. Aztecs everywhere. Was there any way they could gain the upstairs floor? That didn't seem likely, unless they fashioned wings. But with a lull in the firing as the siege settled down to an impasse, Rowdy slipped from his post, leaving Felicia to cover the front of the building, and headed up the stairs. He had a quick look around; from the window of the room Felicia had once occupied, he saw swift, scurrying movement at the edge of the clearing.

Smashing out the glass with his gunbarrel, he sent an experimental shot. He'd gave them cause to believe that the upstairs had defenders, too.

Hurrying back down the steep stairs, he returned to his post not a minute too soon, for Turk had apparently deduced that only one gun was defending the gallery. And Turk had ordered a charge. A dozen vaqueros showed themselves, sprinting hard across the clearing, and Rowdy, hastily reloading, eared back the hammer of the gun and raised the weapon. Then he lowered it again, fired, and the leading vaquero went down, his leg broken. For suddenly Rowdy had no heart in him to kill any of these savage followers of Turk's. Not unless it became absolutely necessary. These were hired hands without a personal stake in the game, loyal and blindly obedient, men who had once served Buck Trimble and now served Gideon Turk. These were savages, acting according to their light. Shooting them would be like shooting a man's horse because you dislike the man.

The one gone down with a broken leg, two others stumbled over him, and Felicia's gun, kicking up dust dangerously near them, sent the vaqueros in wild rout. The charge was broken, Turk's men pausing only to drag their wounded fellow back to the timber; and Rowdy and the girl let them go unscathed. But sometime soon there might be another charge, a greater charge with more men massed for the kill. Gideon Turk would not be averse to squandering his followers. A dozen dead vaqueros in the clearing might mean Halfway House successfully stormed.

Rowdy sighed, then grinned a powder-smoke-begrimed grin at Felicia. "You've never had the pleasure of meeting Abel Karst," he said. "Was a time when I wished he lived in Wisconsin and never left home. But more than once lately I've pined to see his face. I'd like to see him come loping along right now. With Captain Trimble's document to wave in his face, we'd have him on our side. And he's no love for Turk's crew anyway."

Stumpy had left his window to approach Rowdy. "Plumb out of cartridges, old hoss," Stumpy explained. "I heard what you said about Karst. No point countin' on him. I saw him yesterday, on the far side of the ridge. He was headin' south. Likely he's give up the chase and gone back to Bearclaw to roundside. You got any spare bullets, Rowdy?"

Movement in the timber, and Rowdy

raised his gun and clipped leaves from a tree. "Take a look behind the bar, Stumpy," he advised. "This place seems to have been a sort of outfitting post for the mountain country. Shouldn't be surprised but what bullets would be in stock."

Stumpy moved away, and a few moments later sent up a shout. "Plenty of forty-five cartridges!" he whooped and fetched back a few boxes which Rowdy broke open and spilled in a heap upon the floor near the window.

"We can hold 'em," Rowdy judged. "At least till darkness. After that they can be swarming over us before we know what they're up to."

"Hope they don't get the idea of firing the building meanwhile," Stumpy said gloomily.

"I've been thinking about that, too," Rowdy admitted. "Turk wants the sombrero, but actually what he wants is to get Trimble's last will out of it and destroy that paper. Then he can make the earlier will stick. Firing the building would take care of everything for him. Man, if I could only slip through their lines! I'll bet I could talk Abel Karst into riding back here and giving those boys a taste of their own medicine."

"Too bad the sombrero is gone," Felicia

sighed. "With it, you could walk through those vaqueros and they'd never lift a finger."

Don Sebastian, from his post at a window, said, "Would be good time for Quetzalcoatl to show up. He would scare theese *indios* into feets."

"Quetzalcoatl!" Rowdy echoed, inspiration smitting him. "Quetzalcoatl *can* show up! We've got the rig right here."

Don Sebastian shook his head. "I don' theenk it scare Senor Turk or the *malo* hombre with the two teeth steecking out in front."

"What's the difference, so long as it sends those Indians running? Two guns against me instead of twenty or thirty makes better odds. I'm going to put on the outfit and make a try to reach the bar and get aboard my horse. It's our only chance. If I can get back here with Karst before nightfall, the rest of you will stand a show."

Crossing to the bar where he'd placed the false whiskers and cross-bordered robe he'd found in the cellar, he hooked the black beard over his ears and started shrugging into the robe.

"Confound it, Rowdy," Stumpy declared, "you ain't going to galivant off alone to hog all the fun this time. It's my turn to have a hand in this here game. Pass over them whiskers to me, and I'll show you what a god's really supposed to look like."

"But only one of us can go," Rowdy countered. "You've got to help these people hold the fort, Stumpy."

"You can do that," Stumpy stubbornly insisted. "Ever since I've come to this Bearclaw country I've been roundsiding. Fork over them whiskers, Rowdy."

Rowdy sighed. "There's no time for arguing, old hoss. Every minute's got to count if one of us is to get to Bearclaw and back. But I see your point, partner. Let's put it on a fair and square basis." Fishing into his pocket he produced a four-bit piece and sent it arcing into the air. "Heads, Stumpy?"

"Tails," Stumpy countered obstinately.

The coin fell to the floor, heads up, and Rowdy stooped and retrieved it. "Better luck next time, old hoss," he said.

"Confound you for a lucky galoot," Stumpy growled.

"It's all in the way you live, partner. It's all in the way you live."

Outside, the firing had almost died; there was only intermittent shooting as though Gideon Turk had realised the futility of slamming lead into log walls and was awaiting the coming of night. From the window

Rowdy could see no signs of life in the timber beyond the clearing, but he wasn't fooled. The woods teemed with Turk's followers. He wished he knew exactly where Turk and the Gopher Kid were stationed, for those two would not be intimidated by any superstitious dread when Rowdy made an appearance garbed as Quetzalcoatl. But he could see neither of the white men, and he had to take his chances.

The robe wrapped around him and the whiskers in place, Rowdy gestured toward the front door. "Unbar it, Stumpy, and swing it open," he directed. "But keep behind it when you do. I'm going out that way. Wouldn't be dignified for a god to go climbing through a window."

"Good luck, senor," Don Sebastian said softly.

Felicia came close to Rowdy and laid a hand upon his sleeve. "Don't do this, senor," she said.

Rowdy grinned. "Don't worry about me."

"You take keer of yourself, Rowdy," Stumpy said and swung back the door.

Through it Rowdy stalked, appearing on the gallery and pausing for a moment at the head of the stairs. Then slowly and with great dignity he began descending the steps, expecting momentarily that a swarm of bullets would buzz at him from the timber. But there was only silence, a heavy, deathly silence, a silence that seemed to drag out forever, and then a moan rose from the timber, the concerted moan of many men, and the cry went up: "Quetzalcoatl! Quetzalcoatl!"

There was a wild stirring, the threshing of men in frantic flight, and the voice of Gideon Turk reached Rowdy, a wild bellow commanding the vaqueros to stand their ground. Rowdy was steadfastly striding toward the stable, keeping to an even pace when every instinct in him was clamouring that he bolt. A bullet buzzed past his nose; that would be Gideon Turk shooting, and Rowdy fingered his own gun under the robe and wondered if he should retaliate in kind. Would that destroy the illusion of his divinity in those superstitious minds? He paced onward; Turk was firing again, but Turk was also shouting at his followers, trying to stop their retreat.

Now the stable door loomed ahead; a bullet splintered the jamb as Rowdy stepped inside. The Gopher Kid must be on the far side of Halfway House with whatever vaqueros were stationed there, for only the one gun had spoken. Rowdy singled out his mount in the gloom and was glad the horse had been left saddled. Stepping up into the kak, he gave the cayuse a hint of the spurs, and, bending bow to avoid the doorway, came lurching out. Gideon Turk had exposed himself; Turk was standing at the edge of the clearing, shaking with rage, tilting his gun in Rowdy's direction. But a gun boomed from Halfway House, the bullet plucking at Turk's sleeve, and Turk hastily dived back into the timber as a triumphant shout rose from the tavern.

"Stumpy!" Rowdy murmured, recognising his partner's voice. "Good old Stumpy!"

He headed his horse around the barn and into the timber as he had on another occasion when the guns of Karst's crew had bedevilled him, and Stumpy had been at his side.

Into the screening woods, he could hear men moving not far away, but he smiled now, unconcerned. Gideon Turk might be able to stop that wild rout and keep his vaqueros here to hold the others under siege, but Rowdy would bet a pretty penny that no threat or promise would induce those Aztecs to take Quetzalcoatl's trail. The way was clear for Rowdy.

Still, he rode swiftly and with an eye to concealment. A low-sweeping branch slapped at him, wrenching the false whiskers askew. Rowdy paused, removed the beard and cloak and wrapped these articles in his slicker which was tied behind the saddle. Then he sat his saddle for a moment, listening. No alien sound disturbed the tranquillity of the woods in his immediate vicinity. He manœuvred southward a good mile, then struck west to find the main trail that would lead him to Bearclaw. Now the guns were banging again to the north, and by this token he knew the vaqueros had been rallied and the siege was under way again.

God grant that Abel Karst would be in Bearclaw to-day!

The timber thinned, and the main trail was ahead. Rowdy came upon it and rode around a turn. And there, partially screened from view, a man sat his saddle waiting, a gun ready in his hand, and Rowdy, unaware of him until too late, stiffened with surprise. He'd counted his ruse successful, but he'd congratulated himself too soon. The Gopher Kid had anticipated him, and the Gopher Kid blocked the trail.

CHAPTER XV

THE FIRE AND THE POWDER

Whatever kindliness Rowdy had felt toward Turk's vaqueros didn't extend to the Gopher Kid. Not at all. A man might be inclined to spare those Aztecs until it became a case of shoot to kill or do the dying yourself, but the Kid deserved no such consideration. The Kid presumably had centuries of civilisation behind him to impart the finer sensibilities, yet all the Kid had reaped from his myriad ancestry was an inclination toward homicide that manifested itself much too often. At least twice before, the Kid had proved himself more than anxious to speed Rowdy to the hereafter, and Rowdy would have gleefully knocked the segundo from his saddle now with a bullet placed in the vicinity of the Kid's wishbone. The rub was that the situation was apt to be the other way around. It was the Kid who had the drop.

"Hoist 'em!" the Kid urged sharply, and there was nothing for Rowdy to do but obey.

The Kid nudged his mount closer; his free hand reached and plucked Rowdy's gun from its holster. The Kid himself was wearing only one holster to-day, and he made a move to drop Rowdy's gun into it, then seemed to remember that he would need it for his own gun. Rowdy's six-shooter went arcing into the bushes. The Kid giggled, but there was no humour in his cold, close-set eyes; and Rowdy braced himself, expecting this would be the finish.

Within him there was more bitterness than could be crammed into a large barrel, and coupled to the bitterness was a fear that was not entirely for himself. Off to the north, the guns were still banging, the sound muted by distance. Obviously the siege still held. Gideon Turk had stayed behind to rally the vaqueros and to keep them at their deadly work, but he'd sent the Kid to head off Rowdy, knowing full well the Kid wouldn't be frightened of a man posing as an Aztec god. Either that, or the Kid had taken it upon himself to do this little chore and had cut enough sign to realise that Rowdy had headed south. The results were the same. Rowdy had made good his escape from Halfway House, but Rowdy wasn't going to reach Bearclaw and help. The Gopher Kid would see to that. And therein lay the core of Rowdy's fear, for with his failure the defenders of the mountain tavern would be doomed.

The Kid's free hand was groping forward again, patting Rowdy's pockets, and now the Kid's eyes narrowed, and he glanced at Rowdy's saddlebag and then at the slicker behind the saddle. "What did you do with it?" the Kid demanded.

"The whiskers and robe? Rolled up in the slicker."

"I don't mean them. It's the paper I want. Buck Trimble's will. You wouldn't have left it there at Halfway House, not when you planned to walk out. The girl's inside; we saw her. And she had the sombrero. The will is easier toted without the sombrero."

And now, for the first time since he'd walked right into the Kid and his waiting gun, Rowdy saw a chance for at least a temporary reprieve. He'd been about to use his spurs, crash his horse against the Kid's in a blind bid for escape. That such an effort would have likely cost him his life, he'd known. But now some of the tension left him, and he grinned widely. "Did you suppose I figured myself safe just because I got into the woods?" he asked. "Stood to reason some of you might be standing between me and escape. That's why I hid the will once I was out of the sight of your bunch."

Killer lust lighted the Kid's eyes; his gun

raised a fraction of an inch and his finger tightened on the trigger. "I can make you talk!" he snapped.

"Not by blowing holes in me, old son!"

The gun lowered; the Kid gnawed at his under lip with those two large protruding teeth of his. "There are ways," he said ominously. "Slow, sure ways."

A bluff could certainly boomerang, Rowdy reflected. A fine howdy-you-do if he were to be tortured to reveal the whereabouts of a will that might be anywhere, for all he knew. But: "If I lead you to that will, I put Rancho Del Diablo into Turk's hands," Rowdy said. "It's going to take a heap of persuading to get me to do that, Kid. Ranches that size don't grow on every huckleberry bush."

The Kid gave him a slow, appraising look. Then the Kid said, "It's big enough for you and me both, ain't it?"

For a moment Rowdy didn't grasp his meaning — not entirely — and in that moment the Kid pressed his point. "Turk thinks you're just a meddling fool who's fallen for that Mex girl. Me, I think you've been playing for the biggest stake of all — just like the rest of us. Rancho Del Diablo. Getting it will be one thing; holding it another. Buck Trimble found that out. Gideon

Turk's been finding it out. But you and me together . . ."

"Say, you're a cute one!" Rowdy applauded. "And all the time I thought you were sitting your saddle here doing Turk's chores. But you're playing on your lonesome, eh, Kid? Ranch gobbling must be contagious in these parts!"

The Kid shrugged. "We saw you light out. I gave Turk a wave and lit out after you. He figgers I'm down here earning my pay. But supposing that last will of Trimble's was worked over a little so it named *me* as heir instead of the Mex girl. Yeah, Turk told me that Trimble admitted he'd made a new will giving the ranch to the girl. But Trimble might 'a' left the ranch to his faithful foreman — me. Queerer things have happened. With you and me and a worked-over will, Dow, we could grab Rancho Del Diablo, and we could hold it. What do you say?"

Rowdy grinned. "You're like a gent I once met in Seattle who wanted to go partners in the shipping business. If I'd supply the ships, he'd supply the ocean. You're forgetting, Kid. I've got the will."

The Kid giggled. "And I've got the gun."

Rowdy sighed. "Here we are finishing out a circle and bumping into ourselves. What good's your gun? Blow holes in me, and you'll never find where I hid the will."

The Kid's giggle took on a hysterical edge. "But all I've got to do is shoot you and go back and tell Turk the chore is done. Trimble's last will will be the same as destroyed then; it will rot wherever you hid it, for you'll never be able to go back after it. Turk will own Rancho Del Diablo, and I'll be his segundo. It's second pickings, but it's better than none from where I sit."

The gun tilted, lined on a button on Rowdy's shirt, and Rowdy said, with a shrug, "Well, old son, that makes us partners from this minute on."

"Then lead the way to where you cached that will," said the Kid.

"My gun," Rowdy murmured and made a move to dismount.

"Let it lie," the Kid ordered sharply. "We'll come back for it later."

Shrugging again, Rowdy wheeled his horse and headed into the timber to the east of the trail, feeling somewhat bested in the recent battle of wits. There was a certain native shrewdness to this Gopher Kid, and a certain stupidity, too — stupidity that made him all the more dangerous. The wild scheme of the Kid's, for instance, to make himself Buck Trimble's heir had loopholes in it a cow could be driven through! But the Kid had obviously succumbed to the power-fever that obsessed his master, and Rowdy wasn't fooled by the Kid's talk of a partnership. The Kid wanted Buck Trimble's will, and thereafter the Kid planned that Rowdy should die. But at least Rowdy was prolonging his life to this extent.

His only hope was that the slight reprieve might give him some advantage he hadn't had when he'd run into the Kid on the main trail. For he certainly wasn't going to be able to place the missing will in the Kid's hands, and even if he were able to do so, nothing would be changed for the better. That will was in the feathered sombrero, and the sombrero had vanished, apparently into the possession of the mysterious man who haunted Halfway House and sometimes posed as Quetzalcoatl.

Threading through a maze of lodgepole pine, Rowdy felt his hopes ebb. The Gopher Kid was keeping behind him, and whenever Rowdy chanced to glance back, he always saw the Kid's gun in the segundo's hand.

Coming upon a game trail, Rowdy followed it toward the north-east. Off in the distance the guns of siege still banged, the sound intermittent, the sound seemingly no nearer. Twenty, thirty, forty minutes the two rode, and then the Kid's voice rose raspingly. "It can't be far from here. You didn't have time to cover much more country than this."

"We're almost there," Rowdy said, trying to make it sound convincing.

For cold within him was the realisation that his ruse had gained him nothing and that the pretence couldn't be continued much longer. The Kid was already suspicious. And the Kid was giving him no chance at escape. Put spurs to his horse and bolt along the trail? The Kid would knock him out of the saddle before he'd gone ten feet. Turn around and try to get closer to the segundo? The Kid's ready gun would tilt if such an attempt were made.

Yet Achilles had had his heel, and there must be some chink in the invulnerability of the Kid. Rowdy mentally considered his opponent, that curious mixture of shrewdness and stupidity, of avarice and dreams too broad for a pint-sized pair of britches. He had come up against the Kid twice before — once, the other morning when the Kid had hauled him and Stumpy to a cottonwood to die, and again last night when Rowdy had been captured a second time at Rancho Del Diablo after enabling Felicia to escape. On both occasions the Kid had proved himself ruthless and no stranger to violent ways.

Then Rowdy was remembering the appearance of Quetzalcoatl and the wild flight of the vaqueros from the hang-tree's vicinity. The Kid hadn't run then, for the Kid had had no superstitious dread to send him stampeding. Anger had ridden the Kid hard that time, so hard that he'd wildly emptied his gun at the spot where Quetzalcoatl had appeared. Later Rowdy and Stumpy had guaged the distance and realised that it was beyond six-shooter range. The Kid, it seemed, had been showing no more sense than a sheepherder with his pants full of pay. And the Kid had lost control of himself last night, too, when Don Sebastian had serenaded the hacienda with a six-shooter.

Temper! That was it! The Kid had an ungovernable temper, and when it was aroused the Kid let such wit as he possessed fly to the four winds. The cue then was to taunt him to terrible anger and thus perhaps render him impotent, but taunting the Kid under present circumstances was apt to be comparable to tickling a mule's leg to stir the critter. So thinking, Rowdy found that the trail was leading into a small clearing where some wayfarer had made a camp — and not so long ago. The ground was smudged blackly where a fire had been. A few spent cartridges littered the ground, and a few empty tin cans were strewn about. Rowdy swung down from his saddle. "Here we are," he announced.

"About time," the Kid growled.

Rowdy stretched himself indolently.

"Where's that will hid?" the Kid demanded, glancing speculatively at the empty cans.

"I've been thinking," Rowdy said slowly. "Like you yourself pointed out, getting the ranch will be one thing, holding it another. Turk won't take this sitting down. And the Shootin' Soreheads will still be gunning for Rancho Del Diablo, no matter who owns it. I don't think you'll be much help in a tight, Kid."

"So — ?" the Kid said darkly as he, too, swung to the ground.

"I've already got a partner — a good partner," Rowdy pointed out. "Now him and me together could swing a deal the size of the one you've been talking about."

"That stove-up old has-been!" the Kid scoffed. "I know Grampis didn't skip the country like you told Turk last night. I got a glimpse of him at Halfway House. About all he's good for is crow bait!"

"Stumpy might surprise you, Kid. Now

what's to keep me from putting my own name in that will? Captain Trimble was interested in me. I could prove that to a court by showing those advertisements he ran in the Miles City paper. Maybe Trimble, being afraid of Turk, decided to will his ranch to me, since my rep had impressed him. With me owning the ranch, and a gun-handy gent like Stumpy to back my play —"

Anger glinted in the Kid's eyes. "Gun-handy!" he snorted. "All he was doing today was clipping leaves from the bushes!"

"Just the same, he's no .22 calibre fake badman."

The Kid spun his gun so the handle showed. "See those notches?"

Rowdy sneered. "All that proves is that you own a file. Or did you pick that cutter up in a second-hand store, Kid? You didn't show yourself as so very much last night when Don Sebastian blasted at you from the window, out at the hacienda."

"Damn it — !" the Kid began explosively.

Rowdy picked up one of the empty tin cans, paced the full width of the clearing and placed the can atop a rock and then moved to one side. "I've got a right to know what kind of a gun-slammer I'm lining up with," Rowdy said. "Let's see you put four holes in that can. I'll bet I won't be able to cover them with my hand, if you make a hit at all!"

He was holding his breath as he spoke; he'd played the Kid as though the Kid were a violin, building a concerto of fury within him. A fully loaded forty-five held six shots, but those of the hair-trigger gentry usually kept a spent shell under the hammer for safety's sake, so that meant five live bullets. To have asked the Kid to try placing *five* shots in the can, thus emptying his gun, would have been folly. The Kid would have seen through such a ruse at once, and the Kid still wasn't angry enough to be bereft of his senses. But Rowdy's proposal would leave one bullet in the Kid's gun — and the Kid would be remembering that.

The Kid's lips twisted scornfully. "Four shots from here? A cross-eyed could do better than that!"

"Well, you're not cross-eyed," Rowdy conceded tauntingly. "Now just a minute before you start blasting. I don't want to get knocked over by the wild shooting you do." He skipped a half-dozen more paces away from the perched can with a show of concern that was in itself a studied insult. "Take your time, Kid," he urged. "You've got all day."

The Kid's lips drew to a thin line. His

gun tilted, roaring and bucking, the four shots hammered so fast that the sound of them blended into a single roll of thunder, the can leaping into the air and falling behind the rock. Rowdy was instantly at it, and as he reached for the ravaged can, he saw that a silver dollar would have covered the four holes the Kid had put into it.

"Some shooting, eh?" the Kid said self-confidently.

"Just as I thought," Rowdy said, dolefully shaking his head. "The first shot missed entirely. I saw it kick up dust yonder. And with a perched target, too! You'd sure look silly with a moving one, Kid!"

He was walking slowly towards the Kid as he spoke. Now he flung the can high into the air.

And thus did the fire of his taunting reach the powder-keg of the Kid's temper, for suddenly the Kid was as wild as he'd been when he'd emptied his gun at Quetzalcoatl. The hurled can rose, catching the sunlight and becoming a shining, twisting thing, then started its descent. The Kid's gun spoke, and the can leaped upward again, hoisted by a clean hit, then began dropping. But Rowdy was already sprinting hard across the intervening space between himself and the Kid. He was chancing that the Kid had indeed had a spent shell under the hammer to start with. He was risking his life on that chance, but there was no other choice.

The Kid, too late, was realising that he'd been duped. The Kid was pulling the trigger but the gun only clicked, and thus Rowdy knew the gamble was won. The Kid broke open his gun, pawed feverishly at his cartridge belt, and thus his hands were busy as Rowdy reached him. The Kid struck hard at Rowdy with the gun, but, the blow glancing from Rowdy's shoulder, Rowdy got under the Kid's guard, his fist sledging at the segundo's chin.

He hit the Kid twice as the Kid went down, and then he stood over the Kid, his fists cocked, his chest heaving, and his nerves like so many twanging wires. But the danger was over now; the Kid lay prone and unconscious.

Picking up the Kid's fallen gun, Rowdy plucked cartridges from his own belt and reloaded the gun, then dumped it into his empty holster. This done, he thoughtfully contemplated the Kid. Tote him back to Gideon Turk and use him as a hostage in the hope of lifting the siege? Not much chance. The Gopher Kid had been quick to seize a chance to double-cross Turk, and even though Turk didn't know that, Turk would likely be as quick to double-cross the Kid. The Kid, rendered *hors de combat* and thereby a failure, would be so much dog meat as far as Turk was concerned.

Lash the segundo to his horse and tote him to Bearclaw? Here would be proof indeed that Rowdy Dow was no friend of the present master of Rancho Del Diablo — proof that would widen Abel Karst's eyes. But much time had been lost, and the man who travelled the swiftest was the man who travelled alone.

Grinning, Rowdy picked up the diminutive Kid and boosted him aboard his horse, placing the unconscious segundo backwards in the saddle and using the Kid's own lariat to fasten him there. Then, removing the bridle, Rowdy gave the horse a hearty slap. The Gopher Kid was going to return to Rancho Del Diablo in a most humiliating fashion.

The timbered trail swallowed the bolting horse, and soon even the echo of hoofs was lost. Sighing, Rowdy pulled himself into his own saddle and once again faced toward Bearclaw.

CHAPTER XVI

ROWDY DOW — DIPLOMAT

Rowdy, that modern Paul Revere, came across the miles like a homing pigeon outflying a swarm of buckshot; and when in the late afternoon he finally sighted the straggly town, he expelled a mighty sigh. Bearclaw was nothing to write home about, but to-day it looked more enticing than the Seven Cities of Cibola to Rowdy, and he revised the original estimate he had made of the town. A beautiful place, Bearclaw, he decided, so unplanned, so unspoiled, a place for a man to spend his declining years, listening to the babbling brook which sang so soothingly beside the town. Yes, indeed! Thus were Rowdy's perceptions distorted by the remembrance of the angry guns at Halfway House and the need that had sent him beelining to Bearclaw.

Yet Rowdy was far too practical a man to have forgotten that the Shootin' Soreheads, who made this town their citadel, were not likely to greet him with open arms, nor to smother him with affection. Not at first. But there was proof to be placed before them — proof that Buck Trimble, before his death, had turned himself into their friend. The object of Rowdy's mission would first be to place Trimble's document in Abel Karst's big hands, and this endeavour would call for certain diplomatic skill. Therefore Rowdy, after searching his pockets for a reasonably clean white handkerchief and providing himself with a long twig, had fashioned a passable flag of truce.

He rode boldly into Bearclaw, holding this flag aloft, a veritable ambassador of good will, but one who was mindful that the last time he'd ridden this street, the bullets had been buzzing and frenzied pursuit had been shaping up. Now only a few men loitered along the planking, and these stared at him in open-mouthed astonishment, then proceeded to make themselves scarce. Running to fetch Karst, Rowdy judged. He was halfway up the street when the first gun sounded. It broke the twig in its middle and the flag of truce came tumbling down. Rowdy also came tumbling — out of his saddle. Letting his horse bolt, he lighted running, heading for the nearest doorway which, by the very law of averages which prevailed in Bearclaw, happened to be the doorway of a saloon.

More than one gun was speeding him on

his way, but he gained the batwings unscathed, a mighty anger growing in him. A fine way to treat a flag of truce! Then he was remembering that once he'd suggested to Abel Karst that Rancho Del Diablo be approached under such a flag, and Karst had scorned the idea, certain that the bearer would be shot out of his saddle by Trimble's crew. Karst, of course, was convinced that Rowdy Dow worked for Rancho Del Diablo, and Karst had apparently taken to fighting fire with fire. Rowdy, who'd sampled some of the methods of the guarded rancho, could now understand Karst's viewpoint and forgive him for it.

None of which changed the fact that Rowdy was now in need of a fortress, and in this respect he was no different than many diplomats of the beribboned type. Charging into the saloon, Rowdy found only the bartender and three patrons inside. Flourishing his gun, Rowdy shouted, "Out! All of you!" and herded them towards the back door. They went dazedly, stunned by the suddenness of his entry, and he prodded them through the door and barred it after them by tipping a chair under the knob.

Sprinting back to the front of the building, he saw a half-dozen men come charging across the street, and big among them was

Abel Karst. Rowdy sprinkled a few bullets around their feet, discouraging them to the extent that they turned tail, hurrying back to the shelter of doorways and rain-barrels and the slots between buildings. Here they set up a barrage that blasted all the glass out of the front of the saloon and kept the batwings swinging.

Rowdy, crouched low, called, "Karst! Listen to me, you misguided galoot! I'm here to bury the hatchet!"

"Just show yourself!" Karst shouted angrily. "That's all I'm asking. Just show yourself!"

But the invitation wasn't couched in the right tone of voice to be enticing to Rowdy. He ventured near one of the ravaged windows, exposing no more than two square inches of himself, and instantly the guns roared again. Reloading, Rowdy scattered a few more bullets then flattened himself against the wall. A fine howdy-you-do this was. He'd merely traded one siege for another, the difference being that at Halfway House he'd had three friends to help him hold the fort.

"Karst, I've got a paper I want to show you!" he shouted.

His answer was another swarm of bullets, and Rowdy began to grin in spite of himself as the full irony of the situation struck him. He wanted to tell these dispossessed ranchers they might have their land back, and he couldn't make himself heard over the thunder of their guns! Fascinated by the sight of splinters driven from the window sill by questing lead, he was inspired to a bit of whimsey. Scuttling crabfashion to the bar, he helped himself to an armful of whisky bottles, crawled back and began setting these upon the sill, exposing no more than his hand. The next barrage smashed these bottles one by one. "He loves me," Rowdy intoned as the first bottle exploded. "He loves me not. He loves me. Not. Loves me. Not . . ."

He went back for a second load of bottles, and when these fetched another volley, he heard a wild outcry across the street. "He's settin' up all my stock to get smashed," someone complained. "That's what he's doing!" Apparently the saloon's proprietor was one of the Shootin' Soreheads. "For Pete's sake lay off, boys! You want me out of business?"

A lull came in the shooting, which was more than Rowdy had hoped to gain by his mischief. Apparently Karst's crew might unhesitantly spill Rowdy's lifeblood, but they were thinking twice about spilling good whisky. Rowdy was keeping them at bay, and the situation was deadlocked, but how was he to find a chance to surrender to them? Time was running on, and he'd lost too much of it since he'd quitted Halfway House. He raised his eyes above the window sill; instantly the bullets buzzed. Diplomacy was at a mighty low ebb!

On the floor near his hand lay one of the broken whisky bottles. The neck had been sheared off, and the whisky had spilled out. Picking up the bottle, Rowdy, inspired, fetched forth the flimsy letter Buck Trimble had left in a book at Rancho Del Diablo and crammed the letter into the bottle. "Karst!" he shouted. "Have a look at this!" Rearing upward, he flung the bottle across the street; it struck the far planking and rolled towards a doorway where one of the Shootin' Soreheads huddled.

Would they suspect this was a ruse? Would they dare venture forth to pick up the bottle? Rowdy held his breath, waiting. Then an arm was gingerly extended, and when no bullet zipped from the saloon, the owner of the arm grew bolder. A head and shoulders were exposed, the bottle was snatched up, and there was nothing left now but to wait.

A minute passed, five, ten . . . Then

Karst's voice rose. "Dow, if this is on the level, you should be willing to toss out your gun and come walking with your hands raised."

This was more like it! Instantly Rowdy tossed his gun through the broken window and out into the street, and he came through the batwings with his hands hoisted. Stepping down to the street, he stood there while men came converging from everywhere to form a close-packed circle around him. Karst stood scowling, Buck Trimble's document in his hand. "I'm supposed to believe," said Karst, "that the leopard changed his spots just because he saw himself in a wax museum?"

"There's more to the yarn," Rowdy said. "I can spin it if you want. But Gideon Turk has got Felicia Quintera, my partner Stumpy, and a representative of the Mexican government sewed up at Halfway House. I'd like to see you and your boys into saddles. Here's your chance to hit at Turk."

Suspicion still rode Karst; his leathery face was alive with it; and one of his followers was even more sceptical. "Let's lock him up in the cabin calaboose while we palaver about this," the fellow urged. "Me, I think there's a trick here!"

"That coffin-toter's in the calaboose," Karst reminded the man. "And that one window is only boarded up. Maybe between the two of them they'd bust out."

"Coffin-toter?" Rowdy inquired with sudden interest.

"A freighter hauling goods to Rancho Del Diablo. Mostly their supplies are hauled down from the north to miss coming through Bearclaw, but this skinner is new to the country and he took the shortest way. We're keeping him locked up long enough to throw a scare into him, and to plague Trimble a little. Trimble can whistle for the fancy coffin the freighter was fetching in."

"Coffin!" Rowdy exploded and remembered Gideon Turk saying, "Captain Trimble will be buried as soon as a fancy coffin I've ordered for him has arrived . . ." He took a step toward Karst. "That Coffin's for Buck Trimble. He's dead, I tell you; I've seen his body. Part of my job is to prove he was murdered. Who else would they be getting a fancy coffin for but the big boss? Not for one of those vaqueros!"

Karst said slowly, "Buck Trimble dead? Maybe you're telling it straight. The coffin fits in. Spill the rest of it."

Rowdy groaned. He wanted these men up into saddles and taking the mountain trail to Halfway House, but the ways of diplomacy were tedious. He began at the beginning, telling them everything, telling them as swiftly as he could. He explained about the notice in the Miles City paper and how it had fetched him and Stumpy to the Bearclaw country. He spoke of the visit of Gideon Turk to Bearclaw posing as Buck Trimble. Karst nodded significantly at this point.

"One of our boys only got a glimpse of him that day," he conceded. "He saw the feathered sombrero, and that was enough. But he admitted afterwards that the gent who was wearing it looked too skinny to be Buck Trimble."

"It was Turk," Rowdy declared and continued his narrative, telling of the escape from the calaboose and their subsequent capture by the Gopher Kid. "You probably thought he came roaring out to help us, Karst. Actually, he took us up the creek to hang us."

Karst frowned sceptically at the tale of how Quetzalcoatl had appeared and scared off the vaqueros, and Rowdy said, "If your boys caught up my horse after it bolted a while ago, you'll find Quetzalcoatl's garb rolled up in my slicker. But I haven't got to the how-come of that."

He told of Don Sebastian's coming to save them from hanging and of the ruse they had worked then which had enabled Rowdy to get through the fence. He told of seeing Buck Trimble lying in state and of his capture and the effort to escape which had got Felicia free, and of his own subsequent escape with Don Sebastian's help. "We headed for Halfway House and joined Stumpy and Felicia there," he added. "We found the Quetzalcoatl garb in the cellar. When Turk showed up with his vaqueros, I walked through them by passing myself off as the god."

"It jibes with this paper," Karst conceded, frowning at Trimble's document. "Leastwise as far as it goes."

"Look," Rowdy pleaded. "You told me that some day you hoped to get through that fence and have your showdown with Rancho Del Diablo. Here's a chance that's almost as good! Turk's got a lot of the vaqueros off the ranch, and the rest are probably home guarding the fence. Hit at Turk now, and you'll only have half as many to buck when you make your play at the fence. If Felicia gets that ranch, your acreage will be restored to you, just as Buck Trimble wished it at the last. It's your fight too!"

Karst still frowned, but his forehead was

pleated with thinking rather than with anger. The moments ran on, the men stirring restlessly, Rowdy waiting with as much patience as he could command. And then Karst said, "By grab, *I'm for it!* I'm for it, boys! I think this jigger is telling it straight. Up into saddles, fellers. We're riding to Halfway House!"

"Yip-e-e-e!" Rowdy shouted.

Someone had picked Rowdy's gun from where he'd tossed it. The weapon was passed to Karst who held it hesitantly for only a second, then handed it to Rowdy. "Your horse is yonder," Karst said. "Or maybe you'd like a fresh one for the ride."

Thus had diplomacy paid off, and Rowdy was accepted, and now the street was astir with men rushing to such saddles as were at hitchrails, others hurrying to the livery stable for mounts. Rowdy watched all this preparation impatiently; it seemed to take forever for the outfit to get organised, but shortly a score of men were up into saddles and gathering around Karst. But it was then that someone noticed the lone rider who came loping into the street's far end.

"Riding like the devil's spurring him!" the discoverer observed.

"It's Stumpy!" Rowdy ejaculated. "My partner Stumpy Grampis!"

And Stumpy, hauling his horse back on its haunches before the group, was indeed looking as though he'd been trying to outrun his own shadow. Stumpy was haggard with fatigue, but Stumpy was also athrob with excitement. "Rowdy!" he shouted. "We got licked!"

Fear laid a cold hand on Rowdy. "Turk rushed the place?"

"Not more'n a couple of hours after you left! Them vaqueros came swarming from every which direction, and we didn't stand a show."

"Felicia? And Don Sebastian?"

"Turk took 'em prisoners, packed 'em off to Rancho Del Diablo. It's the sombrero he wants, Rowdy, and Felicia swore she didn't have it, told him it disappeared into thin air. Turk just laughed. He figgers the gal took the will out of the hat and threw the J. B. away last night. After he searched all of us, he decided you packed the will with you when you sneaked through his lines. Then he turned me loose to fetch word to you."

"Word? What word?"

"That you'd better turn Trimble's will over to him. You're to come to the pad-locked gate no later than sundown to-mor-row, and you're to come with that will in your hands. Otherwise we'll never see Don Sebastian or the girl alive again. Them's his terms."

Rowdy groaned, but the fury was Karst's. "Damn!" the big man said, his leathery face twisted. "We had our chance, and it slipped through our fingers. Now the whole pack of 'em is back behind the wire again. And they'll be guarding it twice as hard as they were before!"

CHAPTER XVII
GRIM GAMBLE

The Shootin' Soreheads had been lik so many coiled springs, taut with eagerness to launch themselves toward Halfway House. Now the need was gone, and the tension running out of them, they were left spiritless and morose. Quitting the saddles into which they had so hastily piled, they racked the horses with much muttering and began drifting about their business, leaving Abel Karst and Rowdy Dow and Stumpy Grampis standing in the street. Karst was still scowling, a man who'd grasped at opportunity just a trifle too late. Rowdy was reflecting that here was the shape of showdown, for Turk, thwarted, had turned doubly desperate. But Stumpy, having played the role of Sole Survivor up to the hilt and delivered his message, was mindful of an immediate need.

"I'm hungry!" Stumpy complained.

Karst leading the way, the three gravitated up the street to a restaurant and wedged into a booth. Rowdy ordered absently and ate his food as though it were so much sand. A troubled man, Rowdy. His eyes clouded with thought, his cherubic face blank, he munched in silence until the dessert was placed before him. Then he smote the table with a clenched fist, making the dishes jump.

"I've got to get back into Rancho Del Diablo!" he announced. "That's the only chance. I can't bargain with Trimble's will when I haven't got it, so I'll have to find a way to get Felicia and Don Sebastian out of there. But how? Likely Turk has had the fence patched by now."

"We could raise another ruckus like me and Don Sebastian did," Stumpy suggested hopefully.

Rowdy shook his head. "Probably wouldn't work twice, old hoss. Turk's going to be more on guard than ever. There's that Quetzalcoatl garb rolled up in my slicker. It would likely send the fence rider stampeding, but they'd carry word to Turk. And Turk could come god-hunting with a rifle."

"You try getting through that fence alone again," Karst observed, "and they're going to be measuring you for a coffin."

"Coffin . . ." Rowdy mused, then smote the table again. "Karst, you've just given me an idea! You've got that freight wagon here with the coffin for Buck Trimble. Supposing you get down to your cabin calaboose and tell that freighter you're letting him go. Tell him you've decided he's just an innocent bystander and you've got no right to hold him. Then tell him to get out of town pronto. Meantime, I want some holes bored into that coffin so I can breathe. Because when that coffin goes into Rancho Del Diablo, I'll be inside it!"

Karst frowned dubiously. "It might work," he conceded after a moment's reflection.

"It's my only chance!" Rowdy insisted.

"Supposing we leave the freighter in the calaboose, and *I* took the wagon," Karst suggested.

"Too risky. They won't look inside the coffin, but they're sure to flash a lantern in the driver's face."

"Still, I don't like your trying it alone," Karst said. "We've got the boys together now. We could rush that fence."

"If the fence could be rushed, you'd have done it long ago, Karst. Find me a carpenter in this town, and let's get to work on that coffin. I want to be inside Rancho Del Diablo to-night."

"Have it your way," Karst agreed.

They came out of the restaurant with Rowdy rejuvenated, a man in high, hopeful spirits. In the livery stable yard they found the seized wagon, a light affair holding only the coffin which was encased in a rough pine box. A man was fetched who followed the carpenter's trade, and certain explanations were made to him, and he went to work. The pine box was ripped open and the coffin revealed, a beautiful and ponderous thing of carved mahogany. The carpenter toiled with brace and bits, boring a few holes through both the outer and inner boxes on both sides, the three watching him.

"The lid of that rough box will have to be nailed down again," Karst judged. "Whoever passes the load at the padlocked gate probably won't look close enough in the dark to see those holes. But they might notice if the lid wasn't fastened. Your real gamble will be when the coffin is unpacked inside the ranch."

"I'll pile in now," Rowdy said, running his thumb along his belt to check his ammunition. "Go turn that freighter loose. After I've rolled out of here, Karst, you might keep your boys in town and ready to ride. If I get back through and need help in a hurry, I'd like to know where to find it."

Karst extended his hand. "Good luck," he said.

Stumpy, a silent listener up till now, had obviously been wrestling with a mighty thought. "Dang it all, Rowdy," he exploded. "Any way you look at it, it's shore my turn to have the fun. By grab, I ain't gonna be set aside this time while you do the gala-vantin'. It's me that's gonna ride in that coffin! Now don't give me no argument!"

Rowdy, his face the epitome of innocence, regarded his partner. "You're so right, Stumpy," he said.

"That's better," said Stumpy. "Just step aside while I pile in."

"Still," said Rowdy, "I'm the gent who knows his way around the hacienda, since I've been there before."

"I'll ketch on to the lay of the land when I get there," Stumpy countered.

"A couple of lives are at stake, Stumpy."

"All the more reason why a good man is needed for the job."

Rowdy sighed. "There's an argument in favour of my going, and an argument in favour of your going. We could wrangle it out, but we'd be wasting precious time. The only thing to do is put it on a fair and square basis." He fished for the four-bit piece and sent the coin arcing into the air. "Heads, Stumpy?"

"Tails!" Stumpy said obstinately.

"Too bad," said Rowdy, bending to examine the fallen coin in the light of the lantern by which the carpenter had worked.

Stumpy snatched up the four-bit piece and pocketed it. "This is the last time we settle anything this way," he grumbled. "Confound you for a lucky galoot, Rowdy!"

"It's just the way things break, old hoss. Just the way things break."

"Better hurry," Karst suggested.

Stumpy extended his hand. "You take keer of yourself, Rowdy."

"See that my horse gets stabled, partner. And stick with Karst and his boys. If they have to come riding, I'll want you riding with them."

Whereupon Rowdy climbed into the coffin and stretched himself upon the satin lining. The hinged lid was closed, the lid of the rough box put in place, and the carpenter began driving home the nails. A feeling of being smothered smote Rowdy then, and for a panicky moment he was of a mind to call off the entire scheme. But the thought of Don Sebastian and Felicia, remembering that he twice owed his life to the caballero and that the girl had been worth fighting for from the first. And, thinking of them, he stifled his outcry.

There was an interminable wait before anything happened. He heard Karst and Stumpy and the carpenter tramp away, and it seemed forever before horses were hitched to the wagon. Then the wagon started moving with a lurch that almost drove Rowdy's head through the end of the coffin. Jolting along, he forgot his first panic in his efforts to brace himself so as to be comparatively comfortable, and thus the journey to Rancho Del Diablo began.

The released freighter was either imbued with a desire to put Bearclaw rapidly behind him or to recover the time he'd lost in the town, or both. He was apparently flogging the horses with a great deal of vigour. It grew stifling inside the coffin, and Rowdy got his nose as close to one of the bored holes as possible. After a while the road grew less rough, and Rowdy judged they were on the main trail to Rancho Del Diablo. He could hear nothing but the rumble of the wagon. An hour might have passed, or a year; there was no gauging time. After a few jolting miles, Rowdy became convinced that the only way to travel in a coffin was dead. He also became convinced that the driver had got himself hopelessly lost, taken a wrong turn somewhere, and was now in the vicinity of the upper Yukon. Surely they'd passed Rancho Del Diablo miles back!

About then the wagon came to a stop.

Voices murmured, many voices, and one sounded like the Gopher Kid's. The Kid could be back at Rancho Del Diablo by now, Rowdy calculated, if his horse had headed directly for the home ranch. A gate creaked; the wagon started up again, and Rowdy realised they had just passed into the guarded domain.

More lurching, jolting miles. Again Rowdy was beset by his earlier fears. The journey just had to be about over, and yet he was still bouncing along. What was the matter with that fool at the reins? Hadn't he inquired where the ranch buildings were? They must be well toward the north line of Rancho Del Diablo, Rowdy judged, for he would have sworn they'd covered four times the distance between the padlocked gate and the hacienda. Probably he should have stowed some food in the coffin to sustain himself while that loco freighter wandered aimlessly all over creation. He had concluded that he would surely be dead from starvation before the coffin finally lurched to its destination and was opened, and just as he reached this conclusion, the wagon jolted to a stop again.

Another challenge in the night. Another gate creaking. The wagon moved onward but only briefly, rumbling over the tiled paving of a courtyard and coming to another stop. Rowdy plainly heard the splashing of the fountain then. He had reached the hacienda. Voices raised, bare feet padded, and the coffin was lifted from the wagon. Now Rowdy steeled himself, for this was the grimmest part of his gamble, and he took his gun from its holster and held it ready in his hand. Would those who were carrying the coffin notice that it was one hundred and seventy pounds heavier than it should be? He could hear men grunting — many men. A door creaked open; the coffin was lowered to a floor — none too gently. A few minutes later, someone began working at the lid of the rough box with a crowbar. Nails shrieked, the coffin was lifted from the rough box and again dropped to the floor. Rowdy's hand tightened on the gun.

There was more padding of footsteps, a door opened and closed, and silence clamped down. Scarcely daring to breathe, Rowdy waited, silently counting to a hundred. Nothing happened. He counted another hundred. Then he put his hand to the hinged lid and pushed at it, and sat bolt upright in the coffin.

He was in a little room, the room into which he'd peered last night when he'd first come to Rancho Del Diablo, the room where a silent figure lay in state, candles burning at head and feet. Last night there'd been sentries posted inside the room, now there were none. There was only the figure on the dais. The coffin had been placed on the floor, and the rough box had been carted elsewhere.

Rowdy climbed from the coffin and almost collapsed, his stiffened muscles refusing to obey him. Quietly rubbing at his arms and legs, he restored circulation and tried moving again. He took a lurching step toward the dais and stood looking down at the heavy-beaked face, the flowing white hair of the lifeless figure before him. Here, he decided, was the deadest-looking man he'd ever seen.

But how had Buck Trimble died? That was the question, for Rowdy was remembering that part of the job he'd accepted was to determine if Trimble had been murdered and to bring the murderer to justice. Turk had claimed that Trimble had died from natural causes. But last night there'd been sentries guarding this room, both inside and out. Why? Had they been posted to keep those who came to pay their last respects from getting too close to the body and discovering that murder had been done? Steeling himself to a gruesome task, Rowdy fumbled at the shirt buttons of the still figure. A bullet wound over the heart? Rowdy's fingers explored, and he started violently then and whistled softly with the knowledge that was his.

Something stirred in the courtyard beyond. Rowdy whirled, his hand falling to his gun. The wagon was moving again, the gate creaked open, creaked shut — the freighter was making his departure. Rowdy hurried to the door, tested it. It was barred from the outside. He'd expected that; since no sentries were posted at this late hour, the room was bound to have been locked. Crossing to the little window through which he'd once peered from the outside, he found it locked, too. But the catch was on the inside.

Unlocking the window and hoisting it, he crammed his shoulders through the narrow opening, wriggled frantically, worming his way inch by inch. He fell to the ground between the building and the adobe wall, picked himself up and carefully closed the window. There was no way of locking it from the outside, but he was not too concerned about that. Turning, he took a few paces; the hacienda seemed swathed in silence, and Rowdy judged it was well past midnight. Then he was recoiling with horror from the sight that met his eyes.

Back here in the space between building and wall, a cross arm had been erected — Rowdy was sure it hadn't been here last night — and from this crossarm a man hung suspended, his wrists lashed to the bar overhead, his feet barely touching the ground, a man naked to the waist, his back crisscrossed with the marks a lash had made. Rowdy came circling around him and found the man barely conscious, his glazed eyes staring dumbly at Rowdy. These vaqueros of Rancho Del Diablo all looked alike, but there was something mighty reminiscent about this one. And then Rowdy remembered.

"*Por Dios,* senor," the man mumbled brokenly, "cut me down."

Here was the one who'd done sentry duty before Felicia's bedroom door last night and had succumbed to the drugged brandy Rowdy had given him. What was his name? Pedro Montez. Here was the man who'd failed Gideon Turk, and this was the punishment that had been meted out to him. And, staring, Rowdy knew a great anger and a great hate. He was in a sense responsible for this poor devil's predicament, but it had been the cruelty of Gideon Turk that had decreed the manner of punishment, and

Rowdy itched now to feel Turk's scrawny throat between his hands.

He came quickly to the tortured vaquero and fumbled with the knots binding the man's wrists, and when he'd got the knots loosened Pedro Montez fell into a heap upon the ground. Rowdy was remembering Felicia and Don Sebastian again, remembering his duty to them, but he couldn't just let this fellow lie. Besides, here was the makings of an ally, and he might well need one before he quitted this accursed rancho. Stealing quietly around the end of the wing, Rowdy had a look into the rear courtyard.

It lay dark and silent, lighted only by a ghost of a moon, and the windows were so many black blobs. Nothing stirred, and Rowdy ventured to the fountain and began to cup water in his hands until he noticed a gourd set upon the fountain's rim. Filling the gourd, he hurried back to Montez, forcing the water between his lips.

The vaquero opened his eyes; they were less glazed now. Rowdy used the rest of the water to swab Pedro's dark face. The man stirred in his arms, pulled himself to a tottering stand. "Come!" he said and made a move forward, and Rowdy hastily supported him.

Together they came into the deserted courtyard. Montez, stumbling along, nevertheless moved unerringly toward a certain door giving into the hacienda. Rowdy said dubiously, "I wonder if you know what you're doing, old son!"

"Ees chance to escape," the man mumbled and lapsed into a mixture of border Spanish and his own alien tongue, the gist of his speech seeming to be that Rowdy must place blind trust in him.

The door opened to their touch; they were in a dark *galeria,* and Rowdy's companion, groping along, opened a second door. *"Escalera,"* the vaquero said, and they were upon stairs leading downward, stone steps bringing them into the cellar beneath the hacienda. Now Rowdy's eyes were becoming accustomed to the gloom, and he made out huge wine vats. Past these Pedro Montez led him, to the far wall which was made of mortised stones. The vaquero fumbled, seeking a certain stone. He pressed against it, and a part of the wall fell away, for it was a door that now swung inward.

"Ees tunnel, built long ago by El Capitan Trimble," Montez whispered. "Ees built when El Capitan first come here, before Senor Turk has moved from border to join him. Ees not know about thees tunnel,

Senor Turk. Only the most trusted vaqueros, like myself, Pedro Montez, know about thees."

He bobbed into the tunnel, Rowdy hesitantly following after him. Montez fumbled, found a candle and matches placed on a shelf and got the candle aglow. A rocky tunnel stretched endlessly ahead, a natural tunnel which appeared to Rowdy to have once been the bed of an underground river. Rowdy was beginning to understand now. Capitan Trimble had accidentally stumbled upon this tunnel when he'd excavated for the cellar of his hacienda, back in the days before Gideon Turk had come northward to join him. Trimble had kept the tunnel a sccret; apparently even then he hadn't completely trusted Turk. But this Pedro Montez had known.

"Ees way to get out of Rancho Del Diablo," the vaquero explained. "We leave now, senor. I do not ride for a man who uses a wheep on me. El Capitan Trimble, he did not do such a theeng."

"Where does this tunnel lead?" Rowdy demanded, but suddenly he knew where it led; he knew everything now, for the last piece of a puzzle had fallen into place. His fingers closed on the vaquero's arm. "Two prisoners were brought here to-day, Pedro.

Mexicans — a girl and a man. Where are they held?"

"I do not know, senor."

"I've got to stay here, Pedro. But you go through the tunnel. When you're clear of the ranch, I want you to head to Bearclaw and find Abel Karst. You know him? Good! Lead him and all his men back through the tunnel. Will you do that?"

Pedro Montez nodded. "I weel try."

"Think you're strong enough to make the trip?"

"By Quetzalcoatl, I shall find the strength!"

"Good luck!" said Rowdy fervently and came back into the cellar. Pedro Montez must have manipulated some mechanism within the tunnel, for the huge stone door swung shut and became part of the wall, leaving Rowdy in complete darkness.

Groping his way back to the steps, he carefully climbed them and again found himself in the dark *galeria*. He moved along slowly, wondering where to begin his search for the captive pair, and then, suddenly, he was conscious that someone else moved in the darkness. But at that moment a gun-barrel ground hard against his ribs, stopping him short. A match flared and was thrust toward his face, and Gideon Turk said,

"Dow, eh? I wanted a bit of brandy and was coming after it when I heard you fumbling along. Get those hands up, mister; you've troubled me for the last time!"

The gun prodded Rowdy even harder, and he raised his hands in surrender. It had been a round trip, he reflected bitterly. He'd got out of Rancho Del Diablo last night and back again to-night, and once more he was Gideon Turk's prisoner.

CHAPTER XVIII
THE END OF HOPE

The match winked out, and this was the moment for Rowdy to make his play, but Turk was keeping the gun pressed hard against his prisoner, and Turk was lifting his voice in a shout that echoed through the great house. Again Turk shouted, apparently in that weird tongue of the vaqueros, and bare feet padded somewhere close by, a door opened, light showing, and one of the women servants peered at the master of the house. Turk barked a swift command, and the woman disappeared. Not many minutes later she was back with three of the vaqueros.

"Search him," Turk said in English.

Rowdy's gun was wrenched from him, and hands pawed at his pockets, but again they failed to look in his boot top where Trimble's original letter still reposed. One of the vaqueros had fetched a rope, and Rowdy's hands were trussed behind him.

"So you didn't fetch the will along," Turk snapped. "Still trying to run bluffs, eh?"

Rowdy said nothing; he was shoved toward a door and out into the courtyard and across the tiling toward a room in the far wing. Turk, accompanying the vaqueros, produced a key and fitted it into a door, and the door was swung inward.

Into the dark maw of the room beyond, Rowdy was shoved; the door was locked, and the footsteps of Turk and his vaqueros echoed upon the tiling then faded away. Rowdy stood hesitantly, trying to probe the gloom, and heard a faint rustling in a far corner of the room.

"Who's there?" Rowdy whispered.

"It is I, senor. Alvarez."

Things, Rowdy reflected, had come to a pretty pass when there wasn't enough spirit in Don Sebastian Gregorio Jose de Ibarra y Alvarez for the caballero to announce his full name.

"Felicia — ?" Rowdy asked.

"A preesnor in the main hacienda," Don Sebastian said. "We were separated when we were brought here. *Ay de mi!* Eet is a dark and dismal hour, senor."

"It's dark all right," Rowdy agreed. "Are you tied?"

"Only my spirit, eet is fettered."

"Then get this rope off my wrists."

Don Sebastian groped toward him in the gloom, and Rowdy felt the caballero's fingers at his wrists. Shortly the rope fell away.

Rowdy judged that he'd been tied only as a matter of precaution to ensure his not escaping before he was locked in here. He looked about the room, his eyes growing used to the darkness, and saw that it was absolutely bare of furnishings. A heap of straw littered one corner, and upon this Don Sebastian had been reclining. Rowdy tested the door and found it far too ponderous to be shaken by any assault of his shoulder. There was a single window, but it was barred. Apparently this room had been built as a prison cell, and there was no gainsaying that it was a good one.

"What do we do now, amigo?" Don Sebastian inquired.

"We go to sleep," said Rowdy. "The doing is out of our hands. The next move, my friend, is up to Senor Gideon Turk."

"He ees desperate hombre," Don Sebastian said gloomily. Then, hopefully: "You did not come alone, no?"

"I came alone," Rowdy said and explained about the coffin. "Stumpy's in Bearclaw, waiting with Abel Karst. But we've got a chance, Alvarez — a slim chance." He told about the tunnel leading from the cellar, and about Pedro Montez who'd showed him that tunnel and gone upon a mission.

"And thees tunnel, where does it lead?"

"My guess is that it leads to another cellar — the cellar of Halfway House." He dropped his voice to the lowest of whispers. "We never looked behind all those packing cases and barrels in the cellar under that mountain tavern. If we had, I think we'd have found the other end of the tunnel. Halfway House is a long way from here by horseback, but that's because you have to climb up the ridge and down the other side. As the gopher burrows, it isn't so far. The tunnel looks as if it once was an underground river. When Buck Trimble decided to put it to his own use, he probably looked for a place for an outlet. Halfway House was a natural."

Excitement edged Don Sebastian's voice. "That is explain how the feathered sombrero deesappear'. Ees man in tunnel who came into barroom and peecked it up!"

"It also explains why a light was burning in Halfway House the other night when Stumpy and I rode up, but there was nobody in the place when we looked it over. Quetzalcoatl has been using Halfway House as a hideout and the tunnel for quick getaways."

"And Senor Turk knows nothing about thees tunnel?"

"According to my vaquero friend, he

doesn't. Apparently Turk was still down on the border when this hacienda was built. Trimble must have used his most trusted vaqueros for the job and pledged them to keep hush. Trimble didn't trust Turk as far as he could toss a bull by the tail."

Gloom permeated Don Sebastian's voice again. "Eet will take a man on foot long time to get through thees tunnel and then walk to Bearclaw. And weel Senor Karst leesten to a vaquero from Rancho Del Diablo? Weel he not suspect eet is trick?"

"That's the chance I had to take," Rowdy conceded, remembering the flag of truce that had been shot out of his hand. "But I've got one last ace left to play against Senor Turk. It will be a pretty feeble ace, though, since I'm a prisoner. But the point is, amigo, that I know what happened to Buck Trimble."

"You can prove he was keel' by Senor Turk?"

"Maybe these walls have got ears," Rowdy said. "I'll play my ace close to my vest, amigo. You're better off not knowing, anyway. It's the kind of information that could get you killed. Now let's grab some shut-eye. Who knows? Maybe we'll have a busy day."

They stretched themselves upon the straw, but sleep was a long time coming to

Rowdy Dow in spite of the fact that he'd got no rest the night before. His mind seethed with many things, and he heard the even breathing of Don Sebastian long before his own eyes closed. The dawn light, filtering in through the barred windows awoke him; and Don Sebastian stirred at the same time. The two looked at each other ruefully and resigned themselves to waiting.

Within an hour an armed vaquero appeared, fetching them breakfast.

After that the waiting continued; it was nearly noon when the door was unlocked again, and this time it was Gideon Turk who stepped into the room. He stood just within the doorway, tall and cadaverous, and frowned down upon them, his thumbs hooked in a gunbelt he wore, and at last he said, "Well, Dow, I'm giving you one more chance. Where's that feathered sombrero? Or, more important, where is the will that was inside it? The Gopher Kid is here; his horse fetched him back to the gate yesterday. He said he got the jump on you and tried to make you lead him to where you'd hid the will, but you turned the tables. But the point is that you admitted you had the will."

"Just between me and you," Rowdy said with a confidential wink, "I wouldn't trust the Kid too far, Turk. He might try double-crossing you."

Turk's frown deepened. "I'm not afraid of the Kid. Now where's that will?"

"Honest Injun," Rowdy said, "cross my heart and hope to die in a sheepherder's camp, Quetzalcoatl got the sombrero. You remember old Quetzy, Turk? The other night when you were killing me with kindness, you talked about him and said he was something your vaqueros dreamed up. But we found his robe and whiskers in Halfway House, and I used them to get shed of that place. So you see, Turk, somebody *has* been masquerading as Quetzalcoatl. And that somebody got the sombrero."

Turk stroked his chin thoughtfully, and it came to Rowdy that Turk was more worried than he'd ever seen the man. Then Turk said, "You came here last night inside the coffin?"

"Guess," said Rowdy.

"We found holes bored in the sides. You must have come alone."

"Well, there wasn't room for company," Rowdy conceded.

"Someone cut one of my vaqueros down from a whipping post," Turk said. "That was your work, too, I'm guessing. What became of him? He's nowhere about the place."

"Maybe Quetzalcoatl flew off with him."

Anger glinted in Turk's eyes — anger and fear and a new suspicion. "What is it you think you know, Dow?"

"I know you're walking on egg shells, Turk."

Turk said, "Do you think I'd let anything stop me now? There's more ways than one to get around that missing will. There'll be a wedding here this evening. Senorita Quintera has consented to marry me."

His announcement was all the bombshell he might have expected it to be, but it was Don Sebastian who reacted the more violently. The caballero had been reclining upon the straw, a silent listener; now he bounded to his feet, his eyes blazing; but his first lunging step brought a gun into Turk's hand, and Turk barked, "Back you fool! Do you want me to kill you?"

Rowdy said, "So you're really playing it safe, eh, Turk? Going back to the notion you had the first night you met Felicia. Marry her and you're to be master of Rancho Del Diablo. But I don't think you were really able to talk her into *that* notion!"

"She knows both of you are prisoners. She fancies she's in love with one of you.

The price of her acceptance of me is that both of you be allowed to ride away free to-night."

"And you'll keep that bargain, Turk?" Rowdy scoffed.

Turk smiled.

"What do either of you mean to me? It's Rancho Del Diablo I want."

"But there'll be a rifle waiting for us on the trail," Rowdy guessed. "You'd be afraid we'd keep on troubling you. You wouldn't want that. A chore for the Gopher Kid, eh?"

"I've convinced the senorita otherwise," said Turk. "The wedding is scheduled for sundown."

"And will the funeral be before or afterwards?" Rowdy inquired. "Trimble's, I mean. Not ours."

"We shall delay the funeral a few more days," said Turk. "The wedding is far more important."

"Then you'd better put those guards back to work," Rowdy said pointedly. "You wouldn't want somebody to start snooping and find out just how Captain Trimble died."

Turk's eyes narrowed. "Dow," he said slowly, "you insist on digging your own grave with that big mouth of yours, don't you?"

"I just wanted to keep reminding you," said Rowdy, "that you were walking on egg shells."

For a moment a mighty anger gripped Gideon Turk, almost sweeping him away with its intensity. Or so Rowdy judged, watching the man's face. Then Turk strode out of the room, locking the door after him. Don Sebastian began pacing the narrow cell with quick, nervous steps, his face woebegone; and Rowdy, intercepting him, placed a hand on the caballero's shoulder.

"It's not sundown yet," Rowdy said softly. "Besides I think he was bluffing. He can't force Felicia to marry him."

"She would do eet to save the man she loffs," Don Sebastian said dismally. "Eet would be that way with her."

"Hell," Rowdy said sourly. "This is like something out of a damn' book!"

The afternoon dragged its slow course; food was fetched to them again, but Don Sebastian refused to eat. At least four times an hour, the caballero tested the bars on the one window and each time he shook his head sorrowfully. The light grew dimmer until the cell was hazy with twilight; and Rowdy, who'd done much estimating of time and distance throughout the day, began to share Don Sebastian's nervousness. Then a key rattled at the door again, and Gideon Turk put in a second appearance, several vaqueros at his back. The prisoners were ushered out into the courtyard where two saddled horses stood waiting. One was Don Sebastian's bearing the silver-encrusted saddle. The other, obviously for Rowdy, was a Rancho Del Diablo mount.

"You are free to go now," Turk said. "You will be escorted to the padlocked gate and permitted passage through it. The senorita insists on accompanying you that far. Once you're safely through the gate, she will return here to marry me. One of the older vaqueros is a priest among his people. I've looked up the law. There's nothing that says his ceremony will not be binding."

For a moment Rowdy thought Don Sebastian was going to fling himself upon the cadaverous man; and Rowdy moved then, slightly, to prevent the caballero's suicidal play. But Don Sebastian's shoulders drooped, and he walked blindly toward the horse. And the heart went out of Rowdy Dow, too, his last hope dying. There had been time enough for Pedro Montez to have completed his mission, yet the help that Rowdy had counted on had not arrived. Had he guessed wrong? Maybe that mysterious tunnel ran aimlessly to nowhere.

CHAPTER XIX

THE GOD WALKS AGAIN

Stumpy Grampis, that lonesome lamb, had greeted the dawn in Bearclaw with a jaundiced and unenthusiastic eye, a man thoroughly bored with himself. A reliable source has it that he also serves who only stands and waits, but Stumpy was finding confounded little consolation in it. Dang it all, he'd been growing grass between his toes most of the time since he'd come to this mountain country! Rowdy Dow had corralled all the fun by virtue of a flipped coin, not once but three times. Justice was reputed to be blind. In Stumpy's dour opinion, the old gal was also deaf and dumb and too drunk to hit the floor with her scales! Stumpy was fit to be tied.

Last night he'd watched the wagon bearing the coffin rumble away toward Rancho Del Diablo, the recently freed and thoroughly scared freighter at the reins. Then he'd obediently stabled Rowdy's horse and his own as well, and thereafter he'd been Abel Karst's guest. Rowdy, by common consent, had always been the custodian of the partners' funds; and Rowdy, in his haste to get into the coffin, had forgotten to leave Stumpy expense money. All Stumpy had was the four-bit piece he'd picked from the ground after it had been flipped to determine who'd take the ride in the coffin. But Karst had provided Stumpy with a bed in his own cabin, and Karst had left breakfast lying on the table the following morning, but Karst himself had been gone before Stumpy aroused. Stumpy, having eaten, sat in the doorway of Karst's cabin on the outskirts of Bearclaw and brooded.

A dozen yards away, a squirrel ran up the trunk of a tree, perched on a limb and fixed its beady eyes on Stumpy and gave that leathery little man a piece of its mind.

"Aw, go on!" Stumpy said savagely. "You don't have to sit there and tell me what a worthless galoot I am. Go collect some nuts like you're supposed to!"

The squirrel, getting its second wind, warmed to its subject.

"Aw, quit rubbin' it in!" Stumpy growled, and picking a rock from the yard, he hurled it at the squirrel. The rock, inaccurately aimed, struck the trunk of the tree and bounced back, fetching Stumpy a glancing blow on the cheek. Stumpy hauled himself from the doorstep and stalked away from the cabin, the squirrel taunting him until

Stumpy was out of earshot.

Ambling along the town's planking, Stumpy passed a number of saloons, and on the porch of one, across the street, he saw Abel Karst. Stumpy's erstwhile host was talking to several men, and Stumpy was somewhat heartened to find that Karst was still in town. It would just be his luck, Stumpy decided, for Karst to have taken the trail to some excitement leaving his guest in bed. But apparently peace smiled upon Bearclaw, and Stumpy's boredom returned twofold.

Shortly he was abreast of another saloon, and here he fingered the four-bit piece in his pocket, a sudden temptation riding him. By grab, a man was entitled to a drink on special occasions, and Stumpy was certain that if he thought hard enough he could find a reason why this was a special occasion. Still, Rowdy had asked him to stand by, ready and waiting, along with the Shootin' Soreheads, just in case Rowdy needed help in a hurry and came seeking it. But likely Rowdy would ride back with Gideon Turk wrapped in baling wire, the pelt of the Gopher Kid draped over his saddle, and Don Sebastian and Felicia with him, safe and smiling. That's the way things would probably work out.

In any case, a man wasn't going to paint the town even a faint pink on four-bits. Three drinks. The bar-tender might buy a free one then. If it were true that a man grew an extra foot with every drink, Stumpy might emerge from the saloon four feet taller than when he'd gone in. Stumpy climbed the steps and put his shoulder to the bat-wings.

"Just steppin' inside to get the sun off my neck," he told himself.

There was a bar behind which presided a surly-looking individual with a nose by which a man could have lighted his way home on a stormy night. At a few round tables covered with black oilcloth, men list-lessly played at cards, while a drunk slept upon the sawdust-strewn floor. Stumpy emulated a homing pigeon from batwings to bar and slapped the four-bits upon the pine. "Whisky," he ordered.

The barkeep picked up the coin and tried his teeth on it, then turned it over in his hand. "What is this?" he growled. "Trying to pass fake money, eh? This here four-bits has got heads on both sides!" Then, to the men at the gambling tables: "Grab this jig-ger, boys! I think he's having a fit!"

For Stumpy was staring at the coin, his eyes rolling, his slight body trembling, his mouth agape. A coin that said heads no matter which side turned up! Wrath bubbled in Stumpy and threatened mightily to boil up and spill over, and for once even his sulphuric vocabulary failed him. Then he was remembering that each time the coin had been flipped, Rowdy had invited him to say heads, and each time he had obstinately called tails. Just as Rowdy had known he would. Truly an unwary tongue dug pitfalls for a man along life's thorny trail!

Getting a grip on himself, Stumpy stalked stiffly out of the saloon, leaving the coin lying upon the bar. Seating himself at the edge of the porch, he let his feet dangle, his thoughts a crazy quilt of incoherency. A stray cat emerged from beneath the saloon's porch and eyed Stumpy from a distance. "*Mrr-o-o-w!*" the cat said contemptuously. Stumpy was of a mind to heave a rock at the animal, but on second thought decided not to.

Dang it all, it was probably best that Rowdy had taken the ride in the coffin, he finally conceded. After all, Rowdy did know his way around Rancho Del Diablo. But Rowdy could have let him, Stumpy, drive the wagon in place of that freighter. Rowdy had thought the notion of a substitute freighter too risky when Karst had suggested it; but he, Stumpy, would have bluffed his way through at the gate, sure as shootin'. And Rowdy might be needing him at this very moment. His boredom growing, Stumpy pictured himself in the role of a man of heroic endeavour, fighting side by side with Rowdy against the minions of Trimble's ranch. Maybe a man could still get inside the ranch. Maybe they wouldn't be guarding the gate so closely to-day.

Then he remembered the garb of Quetzalcoatl, still reposing inside Rowdy's slicker — remembered the magic it had wrought on two occasions.

Inspired, Stumpy came down off the porch and ambled up the planking toward the livery stable. Three dogs barked derisively at him along the way, but he was deaf to them. By grab, he was going to get in on the fun. And his method was so simple he was surprised at himself for not thinking of it before. Garbed as Quetzalcoatl, a man could storm Rancho Del Diablo lone-handed and come through unscathed. So absorbed was he in this idea that he completely overlooked the fact that Rowdy had considered the same notion last night and decided against it, since neither Gideon Turk nor the Gopher Kid would be awed by such a masquerade. Stumpy was of no mind to fool with petty details.

Into the livery stable, he found the place deserted and quickly saddled his own mount. Then he looked for Rowdy's saddle and found the slicker lashed behind it. Unrolling the slicker, he transferred the false beard and cross-emblazoned robe of Quetzalcoatl to his own slicker. Should he tell Abel Karst about the little expedition he planned? He decided against this. Karst, that practical man, might find flaws in the scheme, and Stumpy liked the scheme the way it was. Or Karst might want to horn in on the fun. Obviously this must be a one-man project — and Stumpy had elected himself to be the man.

Those wire-cutters Rowdy had borrowed from Don Sebastian? Doubtless they were still in Rowdy's saddlebag, and they might come in handy. Stumpy had a look, and, finding the cutters, was putting them in his own saddlebag when he became conscious that a man stood in the doorway, a snaggle-toothed, whiskered man, older than the Rockies and just about as bald on top. The hostler who had once tried to block Stumpy and Rowdy's escape from this same stable. The oldster hadn't been on duty last night when Stumpy had stabled the two horses; now he was back.

"S-a-a-y! Stealing, ain'tcha?" the ancient barked. "Taking them cutters out of some other feller's saddlebag and puttin' 'em in your own!"

"These are my partner's," Stumpy explained and gave the truth a slight twist. "He said I could have 'em."

The oldster peered hard. "Ain't I seed you some place before? Hell on names I am, but I never forget a face. No siree, never forget a face."

"Must 'a' been a couple of other fellers," Stumpy said evasively.

But the hostler, coming into the stable, was moving closer to Stumpy, still peering. "S-a-a-y! Ain't you one of them fellers that busted out of Abel Karst's jail t'other night? You got a nerve, comin' back here."

"Sure, I'm the feller," Stumpy admitted with a sigh. A plague on this meddling Methuselah! "But all that's been cleared up. Ain't you heard? I'm a friend of Karst's now."

"Ain't he-ard nothin'. Been on a fishin' trip, I have. Didn't get nary a nibble neither. S-a-a-y, I betcha they got a reward out for you. Might buy me a new set of store teeth!"

Stumpy was hauling himself into the saddle. Explanations would take time, and, worse, explanations would mean that Abel

Karst would have to be called in for verification. Karst would put this oldster right, but Karst would then be aware that Stumpy had been about to take off on a pasear of his own. And Karst, blunt fellow, might even be so rude as to demand to know where Stumpy was going and what he was up to. A fine howdy-you-do that would be!

Therefore Stumpy, bending low, fed the hooks to his horse and rode straight at the hostler, who veered to one side. Clearing the open doorway, Stumpy looked back and had a glimpse of the ancient diving for the litter of blankets in an empty stall where he kept that tremendous pistol. The gun blasted as Stumpy gained the street, and Stumpy, galloping along, saw men coming to doorways. Abel Karst was one of them. Stumpy gave the man a wave of his hand. "Just exercisin' my hoss!" Stumpy bawled. "He takes off faster if I scorch his rump with a little gunpowder!"

Veering between two buildings, Stumpy hit a trail. And this time he didn't make the mistake that he and Rowdy had made the last time they'd left this town on the run. Stumpy was speeding along the road to Rancho Del Diablo.

But Karst and his crew would doubtless take to saddles and overhaul him to find out what the fuss was about. Still, Rowdy and Stumpy had eluded the Shootin' Soreheads under similar circumstances before, and, by grab, the same strategy would work again. A half-mile out of Bearclaw, Stumpy hauled his horse off into screening underbrush and waited, instantly ready to clamp his hand over his mount's nostrils when pursuit came thundering along. A half-hour passed, an hour, an hour and a half. Stumpy was both impatient and disappointed. He'd left town in a fine glow, exhilarated by the excitement at the livery stable. By grab, that had been a little more like living! But apparently Abel Karst had found out what the ruckus was all about and had decided to let Stumpy go on his little pasear. Pursuit hadn't shaped up after all.

Well, the excitement would likely lie at the other end of the trail. In a mood to grin widely at a squirrel which ran out of a nearby tree limb and chattered at him, Stumpy stepped up into his saddle again, jogged the horse, and set forth once again toward Rancho Del Diablo, not pushing the horse but holding it to a steady mile-eating pace. It was now well past noon and Stumpy became aware that he was hungry and wished he'd thought to fetch along food. Drat that ancient hostler who so persistently speeded the departing guests with a pistol! Stumpy's stomach growled with righteous anger.

He was paralleling that high ridge which he'd twice climbed; to his left Bearclaw Creek flashed in the sun. Shortly Stumpy began to recognise landmarks. About here he had ridden in the willows the other day while Karst and his crew had ridden by on their fruitless quest. Stumpy grinned again. He'd been tempted to call out to Karst then, to seek him as a friend, and now the Shootin' Soreheads were indeed on the same side of the fence as himself. It was a queer world. In his declining years, Stumpy decided, he would write a book proving it was a queer world. A lot of galoots likely weren't wise to the fact.

Soon he was on that straight stretch of road where Karst's crew had once caught up with him and Rowdy and chased them into the arms of the Gopher Kid. Not far ahead would be the padlocked gate, and now Stumpy halted, dismounted, and prepared to transform himself into the feathered serpent god, Quetzalcoatl. The black whiskers he hooked over his ears, and, not having the benefit of a mirror, got them slightly askew. The black robe bordered with white crosses had obviously been tailored for a taller god, and, pulled on over Stumpy's clothes, it flapped most disconcertingly about his heels. Well, a man couldn't expect Lady Luck to have her arms around him all the time. Stumpy hauled himself aboard his horse again.

He'd lost a lot of time hiding out on Karst's crew and the pursuit that had never materialised; and it would soon be night. Yet he held his horse to a dignified walk now; after all a god would hardly go tearing around the countryside like his pants were afire. Rounding a few turns, he then saw the rustic bridge ahead and the padlocked gate beyond it, and disappointment smote him, for there was no one present to challenge him. Reaching the fence, he had a look at the heavy padlock, then dismounted, took the wire-cutters from the saddlebag and fell to work on the wire beside the gate. He had completed the cutting and was about to mount again when a dozen vaqueros came roaring down the road, appearing out of nowhere to dash to the defence of the gate.

Stumpy watched them come, not turning a hair, but in him was the cold feeling that maybe this whole business hadn't been such a sharp idea after all. Then, the riders drawing nearer, Stumpy walked a few paces forward, flapping his arms like a scarecrow come to life.

"Boo!" he shouted.

But now the riders were near enough to be aware that this was no ordinary intruder at the fence. Horses slithered to a stop, the Indians hauling at their reins almost simultaneously, and the cry went up: "Quetzalcoatl! Quetzalcoatl!" For a moment they only stared, seemingly frozen into immobility; and then, as though a signal had been given, they turned as one man and fled.

Stumpy feeling ten feet taller, watched them go, then mounted and rode through the ravaged fence. By grab, this was more fun than a barrel of chipmunks! Too bad he didn't have some of those skyrockets from Halfway House. With fireworks shooting from either hand he'd show those vaqueros how a first-class god put on a show.

The road wound northward into the folding land. Doubtless the ranch buildings lay at the end of the wagon ruts. Stumpy's urge was to hurry, but he remembered the dignity that went with godhood and kept the mount to a walk. Already those stampeded vaqueros were lost from sight. Well, shortly Stumpy would be at the ranch and he'd wave his arms a few times and say *"Boo!"* again, and Turk's vaqueros would be falling over each other getting out of his way. Rowdy would be saved from whatever predicament he happened to be in, but Stumpy would be right tolerant about the whole thing.

" 'Tweren't nothin', old hoss," he'd say. "Just a notion and the guts to go through with it, that's all it took." He hoped Rowdy would have the good grace to blush.

Immersed in his thoughts, he was aware that a clump of trees and bushes bordered the road just ahead of him, on a rise of ground that overlooked the fence and the road beyond the gate, but those trees couldn't conceal more than a dozen riders, and Stumpy was frankly disappointed. He was hoping for greater opposition to give a zest to this thing, and he didn't see the *one* man until he was almost on top of him. The Gopher Kid, that artist at ambuscade, sat his saddle in the depth of the little grove, and he had a ready rifle trained on the trail. He said, giggling, "Raise your hands, mister!"

Too late did Stumpy try clawing for his gun. That confounded robe got his hand all snarled up. The Gopher Kid nudged his mount and rode out; still keeping the rifle lined on Stumpy's brisket, he reached and got Stumpy's gun and thrust it into his own belt. Then the Kid looked toward the lowering sun, shifted his gaze to the north, and apparently made some silent calculation of time and distance. "Now," said the Kid, "we'll be going on to the ranch."

But Stumpy, submerged in gloom, scarcely heard him. Two men on this whole spread who weren't apt to be impressed by an Aztec god, and he'd had to run smack dab into one of them! Only then did he begin to wonder why the Gopher Kid had been stationed here, a rifle ready. It had all the earmarks of an ambush. But for whom? Surely the Gopher Kid couldn't have known that Stumpy Grampis would be coming.

CHAPTER XX

TRIGGER TEMPEST

They were there in the courtyard at Rancho Del Diablo, Rowdy Dow and Don Sebastian and Gideon Turk and a half-dozen vaqueros, and there was nothing left now but for Rowdy and the caballero to mount and be escorted safely to the padlocked gate. Such was the bargain Felicia Quintera had struck with Turk, and there was scant consolation in it for either Rowdy or Don Sebastian. Beyond the gate, Rowdy was sure, an ambush would be awaiting them, yet his greatest fear at the moment was for his Mexican friend. Don Sebastian had turned desperate, and even though the caballero hauled himself into his silver-encrusted saddle, a man stunned, Rowdy wasn't sure but what Don Sebastian would yet hurl himself upon Turk. The trouble with Mexicans was that they used too much pepper in their food. It got into their blood.

Gideon Turk said, "Senorita Quintera will be along in a few minutes, and then we shall start."

One of the vaqueros spoke swiftly in his

alien tongue, and Turk lifted his eyes in surprise to the wrought iron gate in the adobe wall. Someone fumbled at the gate, unlocking it; the gate swung inward and two horses moved into the courtyard, the Gopher Kid astride one, his rifle held ready, Stumpy Grampis, or a reasonable facsimile thereof, aboard the other mount, for Stumpy still wore the robe of Quetzalcoatl, the black whiskers hanging more askew than ever on his leathery face.

"Quetzalcoatl!" one of the vaqueros muttered and turned to bolt.

"Stop, you fool!" Turk commanded. "Can't you see that it is only a man garbed as a god!" Then, to the Kid who'd hauled his horse to a halt: "Where did you find him?"

"He cut the fence at the gate," said the Kid. "Some of the vaqueros saw him, but they were scared out. I waited in the trees till he was near enough and got the drop on him. I figgered there was time enough left to fetch him here." He giggled. "I had a notion to shoot him. But there was always the chance that you might be on the road with the senorita."

Turk nodded. "She wouldn't have liked running into that," he conceded. "I suppose she'll count Frumpit into the bargain, too."

The vaqueros were still eyeing Stumpy with a mixture of suspicion and dread, and Turk walked to where Stumpy sat his saddle. Reaching, Turk wrenched the false whiskers from Stumpy's face. "Do you see?" he demanded loudly. "He's only a man!"

A vaquero made some sort of protest in his own tongue, and Turk said angrily, "Of course he isn't the one who appeared at the time you tried to hang this one! That was somebody else wearing the same whiskers and robe. And Dow, here" — he jerked his thumb at Rowdy — "wore the outfit at Halfway House yesterday. Don't you fools understand? Each time it has been a man who has pretended to be Quetzalcoatl!" He tore the robe from Stumpy and flung it to the tiled paving. "The god shall walk no more!"

Stumpy raised rueful eyes to Rowdy. "I tangled my twine, Rowdy, old hoss. The idea was a good one, but it didn't work. It got me through the fence, but this buck-toothed son was waiting in the trees — waiting to ambush *somebody*. He got the drop on me afore I could bat an eye."

A door giving from the main part of the hacienda opened and Felicia stepped into the courtyard, one of the native women at her elbow. The girl was still garbed for the trail, and her face was the more beautiful in its sadness. She looked from Rowdy to Stumpy to Don Sebastian, smiling faintly, and then to Gideon Turk, and her smile faded. "I am ready, senor," she said simply.

And suddenly Rowdy was sick of scheming and pretence, sick of waiting and hoping and tasting futility, sick of Gideon Turk and his machinations, and goaded to a recklessness that was suicidal. He had hoped to stay Don Sebastian's impetuousness, and his own ran away with him. He said loudly, "You don't have to go through with this, Felicia, and you'd be a fool if you did. The Gopher Kid just captured Stumpy near the gate. The Kid was posted there with a rifle, savvy? Either he was to pick us off once you thought we were safely through the gate, or else he was to follow and do that chore as soon as possible. Turk wouldn't play fair with his own grandmother!"

Anger darkened Turk's bony face, and he took a step toward Rowdy. "I told you, Dow, that you'd dig your own grave with that big mouth of yours!"

The Kid's giggle was a sharp, insane thing. "Let me!" he insisted eagerly, his gun levelling at Rowdy. "Let me, Turk! You ain't forgot about him tying me backward on my own horse?"

"Get it over with!" Turk barked.

A gun roared, the thunder of it filling the courtyard, and Rowdy, who'd braced himself for the shock of the bullet, saw the Gopher Kid flinch, dust spurting above the left pocket of his shirt. The Kid sat his saddle for a moment, his eyes glazing, the gun in his hand exploding harmlessly from some last reflex, and then he was falling from his saddle. A gun spoke again, and another echoed it, and men came bursting from the same doorway by which Felicia had entered the courtyard, a dozen men, and one of them was Pedro Montez, and one was Abel Karst. And Rowdy, seeing the broad face of Karst, grim above a six-shooter, cried jubilantly and with understanding: "The Shootin' Soreheads!"

Pandemonium reigned in the courtyard, horses squealing and pitching, vaqueros unleashing their own guns to meet the attack of Karst's crew, and it was a veritable trigger tempest. A man couldn't have stirred up more excitement if he'd taken all the fireworks from the cellar of Halfway House and lashed them under the bellies of the horses.

Rowdy leaped upon the nearest vaquero, clubbing at the man with his fist and wrenching the fellow's gun from his hand as the vaquero went down. Stumpy, a wild delight in his eyes, was launching himself from his horse upon another vaquero, and Don Sebastian, alive now with hope, was looking around for an adversary.

"Get to Felicia!" Rowdy shouted at the caballero. "Get her out of harm's way!"

Don Sebastian, his teeth flashing in the first smile Rowdy had seen him wear to-day, began fighting his way to where Felicia had pressed herself against the hacienda wall, the native woman cowering beside her. Men had come to grips, and the courtyard was filled with writhing figures locked together, but some were still free-handed to use guns, and the guns continued banging. Vaqueros were pouring from the doors giving from the wings of the hacienda, and two of them leaped upon Rowdy simultaneously, giving him a busy moment. Stumpy relieved him of one adversary by the simple expedient of bending a captured gun over the head of the man. Rowdy had just taken the feet from beneath the other by a looping blow to the man's jaw, when Abel Karst came panting up.

"What happened to you?" Karst barked at Stumpy. "You couldn't have been ten minutes gone from town when that vaquero showed up. But we couldn't spend time looking for you, when we had to get into saddles."

"You believed Montez right off?" Rowdy asked.

"Those whip marks were pretty convincing proof that he had no reason to love Gideon Turk. The poor devil was just about done in, but we headed right back to Halfway House with him, fetching lanterns along. The tunnel slowed us down. It must be several miles long, and we had to go on foot."

A vaquero careened against Karst who flattened the man with his huge fist. "What's the odds against us, Dow? I managed to round up about twenty to ride with me. The rest are inside the house, taking care of any trouble there."

"Some of the vaqueros are out on the range," Rowdy judged. "How many, I don't know. It looks like the odds are about even here. But those others will hear the guns and come loping. We've got to clean up things here fast and get the gate in the wall locked. The Gopher Kid had a key. Search his clothes. And Turk's likely got one, too."

"Turk!" Karst barked. "Where is he?"

For Gideon Turk was no longer in the courtyard, as Rowdy saw by a quick look around. Turk had managed to disappear in the confusion, and Rowdy said, "I'm heading into the house! Send some of your boys to search the wings, Karst. He's the kingpin, and we've got to root him out!"

Whereupon Rowdy darted for the nearest door, let himself inside the main hacienda and made his way into the big room where once he'd been entertained by Gideon Turk. Here he found overturned furniture and sprawling vaqueros and three of the Shootin' Soreheads prowling about with ready guns. Also he found Felicia here, fetched by Don Sebastian who'd apparently returned to the courtyard to have a hand in the fray.

"Seen Turk?" Rowdy barked, and when all shook their heads, he ran through the nearest doorway. He came along a hall, a trifle lost in the confusion of this great house, and he found an open door giving from this hall. Steps led downward into the cellar, and Rowdy ventured upon these steps, sure now that he knew where Gideon Turk had fled.

The entrance to the tunnel! Turk was going to make his escape through the tunnel! But no, Turk hadn't known about the tunnel. Turk, then, had merely chosen the cellar as a place to hide himself. But supposing Karst's crew had left the tunnel door open and Turk found it? Rowdy quickened his steps, and almost paid dearly for the unwariness made of haste. Gunflame lighted the cellar's gloom, and a bullet zipped past Rowdy's ear.

But Rowdy was now to the bottom of the stairs, and he flung himself full length upon the stone floor. To his left were the wine vats, and Rowdy scuttled on hands and knees to the shelter of one of these, the sound of his movement drawing another bullet. But now he'd located Turk. The man was deep in the cellar, down toward the wall where the tunnel began, and Turk had stationed himself behind some barrels which stood in a dusty corner.

"The game's all played out, feller!" Rowdy shouted. "Better toss away your gun and come out with your hands up!"

His answer was another bullet which bored into the wine vat, the wine beginning to pour from the hole. Rowdy craned his neck; the door to the tunnel had indeed been left open. Surely Turk had noticed this and deduced how Karst's crew had gained entry to the hacienda. But Turk hadn't quite had time to reach the tunnel, and now Rowdy had the man penned up. But Turk would be doubly desperate for that very reason.

"Rowdy?" That was Stumpy speaking at the top of the stairs. "You down there, Rowdy?"

"Stay back, Stumpy!" Rowdy warned him. "Turk's here, too, and he can cover the stairs!"

"Karst said to find you, Rowdy, and tell you he got a key to the gate. The Gopher Kid had one on him. But about twenty more of them Injuns are loping across country toward these buildings. They'll scale the wall, shore as shootin'. Some of the rest are still hid around the house. We're going to be outnumbered mighty pronto."

Turk, behind the barrels, said jubilantly, "It's you who'd better be throwing down your gun, Dow. It's going to be a wipe-out in the long run — a wipe-out of you and your friends."

Which was exactly the thought that was tormenting Rowdy. He'd guessed right last night about where the tunnel led, and Pedro Montez had been successful in persuading Karst to fetch his crew into Rancho Del Diablo by means of the tunnel. They'd arrived just in time to save Rowdy's life, and they were practically in command of the hacienda now, but the balance might quickly swing the other way. Once Don Sebastian had claimed that a hundred men rode for the ranch. Those men would be coming, drawn from calf-branding and fence-patrolling and whatever else kept them out on the range, drawn by the sounds of gunfire or by fleet messengers hurrying from those outside the wall to those in the remote corners of the ranch, drawn for a final assault that would put Rancho Del Diablo back into Turk's hands.

"Stumpy, how about that Quetzalcoatl outfit?" Rowdy called. "Can you put it on again and post yourself on the wall? That will stop any vaqueros from the outside."

"No good, Rowdy. The outfit got all trampled by the hosses when the ruckus started. Them whiskers is plumb ruined."

Turk laughed harshly. "You're running out of luck," he shouted. "Better surrender, Dow!"

"I'm coming down there!" Stumpy cried angrily. "I'll give you a hand at tacking that galoot's hide on the wall!"

"No, Stumpy!" Rowdy shouted, aghast. "Don't try it!"

But Stumpy was already upon the stairs, exposing himself to Turk's gun, and Rowdy desperately reared himself upward and stepped out into the full view of Turk, firing as he did so. Turk jack-in-the-boxed upward from behind the barrels, his gun blazing, the thunder of it echoing weirdly in the confines of this cellar; and Rowdy felt a bullet pluck at his shirt. And then Rowdy became aware of the man who was emerging from the tunnel, the man who stood framed in its open doorway. He had only an impression of bigness, of a breadth of shoulders and of the feathered sombrero the man wore — these and the man saying softly, "Here, Turk — !"

Gideon Turk spun, catching his first glimpse of the man, and fear was in Turk's eyes, but hate flamed there, too, and Rowdy, seeing all this, stayed his own fire. The gun in Turk's hand swung toward the tunnel door and bucked, but it had been fired a fraction of a second too late, for flame had leaped from the direction of the tunnel entrance. Turk took two hesitant steps forward, tripped blindly over some debris on the cellar floor, and fell face forward, dead. Thus did his dream of power end, here in the dirt of the cellar of the great hacienda he had coveted.

Rowdy looked toward the man with the feathered sombrero. "I figured you had the most right to him," Rowdy said. "I'm Rowdy Dow."

Stumpy was halfway down the steps, and here he paused peering hard and letting his jaw fall in surprise. Behind him Abel Karst suddenly loomed, his voice raised to an angry bellow. "Dow, is that you down there?

There's something in this place that's mighty crazy, and I want to know about it! I was just looking in one of the wings, trying to hunt down Turk. I found a figure laid out with candles burning — a figure that looks exactly like Buck Trimble. But it wasn't him — *it was a wax dummy!*"

"Yes, I know," Rowdy said. "A dummy that Captain Trimble first saw in a waxworks museum in San Francisco, along with figures of some mighty unpleasant boys. It was seeing that dummy that made Trimble see himself as others saw him. My guess is that he bought the dummy so it wouldn't be on display, then had it sent here so he'd have it to remind him of what he'd once been. But you can ask him yourself. Look hard, Karst. See who's standing in the tunnel door."

Karst's surprise was as great as Stumpy's. "Captain Trimble!" he gasped.

"In the flesh," said Rowdy. "Come out, Captain. The palaver can wait till later. Right now you'd better go upstairs and show yourself and that feathered sombrero at the gate. The sight of it should stop those boys of yours who are probably climbing over the wall right now. This, I reckon, will wind up the show."

CHAPTER XXI

FIESTA AND FAREWELL

The great hacienda blazed with a hundred eyes, light springing from all the grilled windows to fall upon the courtyard, and in the huge room where Rowdy had once dined, the ornate furniture had been shoved to the walls, and stringed instruments and castanets and rattling gourds urged all to the tango, for this was fiesta. Out in the courtyard where men had fought desperately only a few hours before, the Shootin' Soreheads strolled among Trimble's vaqueros, making their peace, for the fighting was done with. The feathered sombrero had wrought its magic, just as Rowdy had judged it would, and Captain Buck Trimble again commanded Rancho Del Diablo.

From the merriment, Rowdy Dow had removed himself; he had gone beyond the wrought-iron gate where Trimble, fetched from the cellar after the death of Gideon Turk, had stood with arms upraised and stopped the charge of the vaqueros. Perched upon the top of an adobe corral, Rowdy, freshly shaved for the first time in several days and looking bright as a new button, was letting his feet swing, and seated beside him was Abel Karst. Buck Trimble stood below them, a heavy-beaked, silver-haired man, the feathered sombrero cocked back upon his head, a cigar blowing in his face. He was smiling a contented smile, was Trimble, but Karst, not yet at ease with his long-time enemy, scowled a scowl of bewilderment.

"I've put some of the pieces together," Karst said. "But there's still things I don't savvy. A wax dummy — !"

"It's all simple enough," Trimble said. "Dow, here, tells me you saw the paper I prepared and left hidden for him. So you know that I intended to make restitution to you and the others. I almost signed my own death warrant when I let Turk know of my intentions. Turk was determined to be master of the rancho, and Turk knew that my original will made him my heir. So Turk wanted to lay his hands on the second will — the one that gave the ranch to Felicia Quintera. He wanted to get that will and destroy it. Also, he had to destroy me."

Trimble's glance shifted to Rowdy. "Perhaps you wondered, Dow, why the notice I put in the papers directed you to meet me in Bearclaw rather than at the ranch. Now you understand."

Rowdy nodded. "Bearclaw was dangerous for you, but it wouldn't have been safe for you to have talked over your notion with me out here at the ranch. Not with Turk around."

Trimble nodded, too. "My life had ceased to be safe once I'd told Turk about my plans. The question was whether I'd live till you arrived. I'd sewed the second will inside the feathered sombrero and advised the Mexican government of this at the same time that I asked them to help locate Senorita Quintera. To play double safe, I prepared the document for you which I left in my library, and I arranged to have a note put into your hands in Bearclaw. Not long after that, I was fired upon here on my own ranch. The Gopher Kid was behind that little ambush, I imagine. It was a miss, but it was close enough to knock the feathered sombrero from my head, and I lit out, letting it lie. That's how Turk got the sombrero. I was scared enough that I decided to leave the ranch."

"By way of the tunnel," Rowdy guessed.

"That's right, Dow. I'd had that tunnel prepared when the house was first built; I only had to fashion an entrance and an exit at the time, since it was a natural tunnel. I arranged with the proprietor of Halfway House to have the exit in his cellar, paid him well and swore him to secrecy. When I quit Rancho Del Diablo, I left through the tunnel. Since then I've been using Halfway House as a hideout."

Rowdy said, "I savvy now that it was you who were there the night Stumpy and I saw the light burning."

Again Trimble nodded. "After I chose to disappear, Turk must have got the notion to make believe I was dead and proclaim himself master of the ranch under the provisions of the first will. He had to have a corpse to convince the vaqueros, and he remembered that wax figure. You guessed right, Dow, about my buying it from the Frisco waxworks. I didn't want it on public display, so I bought it and had it shipped here. I always meant to destroy it, but it lay around in a packing case for a long time. None of the vaqueros had ever seen it — but Turk knew it was here. All he had to do was alter the eyelids so the eyes appeared closed — a little careful work with a paint brush did that, I imagine. Then he had the dummy put into a guarded room, allowing the vaqueros to see it but making sure that none of them got too close to it."

"I found out the truth last night," Rowdy said. "I'd never supposed for a minute but what it was your body, but I had a close look-see because I wanted to know if you'd been murdered. That was when I learned the truth. That gave me an ace-in-the-hole to use against Turk, but it wasn't much of an ace as long as I was Turk's prisoner. To-day he was afraid I'd guessed everything, which was all the more reason why he wanted me dead."

"But this business of your passing yourself off as an Injun god — ?" Karst interjected, glancing at Trimble.

Trimble grinned. "I've always had an intense interest in things pertaining to the Aztecs, and it was no trouble to provide myself with the garb of Quetzalcoatl. I'd had it prepared as a joke quite some time ago, and stored it away in my room. One night I came back into the hacienda through the tunnel. What I wanted was the feathered sombrero, since the second will was hidden in it, but Turk was keeping the sombrero close to him day and night since it gave him authority over the vaqueros. When I couldn't get the sombrero, on impulse I took the garb of Quetzalcoatl instead. After that I made appearanccs in it from time to time. The vaqueros supposed they were seeing the god, but I knew that when they reported the matter to Turk, he'd know better. Turk would guess that it was I who was masquerading as Quetzalcoatl."

"I see," Rowdy said slowly. "You were working on Turk's nerves, reminding him that you were still alive and close by and that his scheme to make it appear that you were dead had a big hole in it. But why didn't you show *yourself* to the vaqueros? They'd have had to savvy then that there was something loco about your body being on display."

"You forget their superstitious minds, Dow. They'd have only presumed they were seeing my ghost, if they'd actually seen me moving about. Turk might have talked them into trying their guns on a ghost. But I knew they weren't going to shoot at Quetzalcoatl! They were only going to turn tail and run when they saw one of their gods."

"That's right," Rowdy agreed, remembering the wild stampede he had witnessed at the hang-tree. "I can savvy now why the Gopher Kid tried shooting at you the day you came along when me and Stumpy were about to be hanged. The Kid knew damned well who the vaqueros had seen!"

"From the slope, I watched the Kid bring you and your partner to the cottonwood,"

Trimble said. "I didn't know who you were, but I broke up the play anyway. Afterward I started working my way down on foot to free you. When I got close, I saw you riding off with the fancy-dressed Mexican. That was the second time I'd just missed you by a narrow margin. The night before I'd been having something to eat when you and your partner rode up. But I headed for the tunnel as soon as I heard your horses. It might have been Turk coming, or Karst, here. I couldn't take chances."

"And you were in the cellar when Felicia fetched the sombrero to Halfway House a couple of mornings later."

"That's right, Dow. I heard voices. Since talking to you earlier to-night, I realised now that those voices were Felicia's and your partner's. But I had no idea Felicia was in Montana. When they went out to the stable, I ventured into the barroom. There was the sombrero upon the bar. I snatched it and ran into the tunnel. I'd gotten my hands on the will Turk wanted so badly, but I didn't realise that I was taking the will from the one person in whose hands I wanted it placed — Felicia Quintera. I headed deep into the tunnel, and when I finally ventured back into the cellar of Halfway House late that night, I discovered that someone had taken the Quetzalcoatl garb. That was you, of course."

Rowdy sighed. "Too bad we never got to the same place at the same time."

"I figured you might be in the country," Trimble said. "I even thought of trying to meet you in Bearclaw, as I'd told you I would, dangerous as it was. But I'd told you that you'd know me by the feathered sombrero I'd be wearing. And Turk had the sombrero. So I took a chance that you'd follow up on the note I'd left with that kid from Bearclaw."

"You weren't in the tunnel to-day, Trimble," Karst observed. "Not when we came through."

"I was snatching some sleep in one of the beds at Halfway House," Trimble explained. "I heard the horses when you and your crew came galloping up. You didn't look around; your only thought was to follow Montez into the tunnel, and when you all went through, I knew that something big was shaping up. I followed after you. The rest you know."

Rowdy grinned. "All that fuss over a will, and the man who wrote it was alive all the time!"

Trimble knocked ashes from his cigar, his heavy-beaked face softening. "You worked for me, even when you thought I was dead, Dow," he said. "Because of what you did, I'll be able to carry out the plan I made when I had my change of heart. That's why I paid you the balance of the ten thousand dollars to-night. You earned it."

"Well, there were some expenses," Rowdy conceded, remembering the saloon-keeper in Bearclaw who'd had his stock thoroughly salivated. "You'll be running your ranch again, Captain?"

Trimble shook his head. "I'm going to Mexico soon, to live out the rest of my years. I lived there so long I'm half Mexican anyway — or Aztec, if you like. Karst, Senorita Quintera will be boss of this ranch from now on. And the acreage that was taken from you and your friends will be restored as soon as the legalities can be attended to. I'd like to offer my hand."

"And I'd like to take it," Karst rumbled, coming down from the corral's top and extending a huge paw. "You gave us a good fight in your day, and we gave you a good one in return. I can see now that a lot of the deviltry we laid at your doorstep was really the doings of Turk and the Gopher Kid. You're squaring things up now; that's all any man could ask."

Trimble glanced at Rowdy. "Felicia tells

me she's offering you the foreman's job here, Dow. Will you be staying on?"

Rowdy sighed. "I reckon not. The real work's done, Trimble. I'll be hitting the trail as soon as I can collect my partner. Stumpy wanted to be in on the fiesta."

"Here he comes now," Karst observed.

The little man was weaving toward them unsteadily, his voice raised in a song that was more words than music and had something to do with a certain Lizzie who was a lady, although her past was shady. Stumpy lurched to a stop near the corral and regarded the three owlishly. "Gonna be a wedding, old hoss," he said. "Don Sebastian and Felicia. They just told me."

Rowdy nodded. "I guessed as much. Turk said that Felicia had agreed to marry him if he'd free me and Don Sebastian because she was in love with one of us. I never had any doubts about which one it was."

"Can't blame her," Stumpy said thickly. "Can't blame her a-tall. I'd do the shame — same thing in her place. Couldn't expect a lady to wansh to be plain Mishus Dow when she could be Mishus Don Jose Gregorio Sebashian Alvaresh Ibarrish."

"Stumpy!" Rowdy ejaculated in understanding. "You've been at Captain Trimble's brandy. The Napoleon 1814."

"Wash it that old?" Stumpy said in surprise. "Hey, Cap, why don'sh a rich galoot like you have shomething newer around the shebang?" His gaze wavered, found Abel Karst. "Ain't gonna be no more Shootin' Soreheads now," Stumpy observed solemnly. "Got to getsh a new name for the organizashun. I know! Call 'em the *Shatisfied* Shoreheads, thash what. How do you like that? The Shatisfied Shoreheads." He fell to singing again.

Rowdy reached for a lariat that lay atop the corral wall. "Stumpy," he said sternly, "I'm going to have to tie you in your saddle."

"We goin' shomeplace?" Stumpy demanded. "Me, I wansh to tango shome more." He executed a couple of dance steps and snarled up his legs, falling in a heap. When he'd pulled himself to a stand again, he said, "Very well, Rowdy, old hosh." His bleary gaze fell upon Karst and Captain Trimble. "I'll be ready to ride shoon as I shake handsh with these four gentlemensh!"

"That should keep you busy for a while," Rowdy decided. He ran his hand over his freshly-shaven chin, "Me, I'm going inside the hacienda to kiss the bride. Damned if I'm not."

A half-hour later the two sat their saddles

atop the rise of land where Rowdy had first looked upon the buildings of Rancho Del Diablo, and again the adobe glimmered white in the faint moonlight. But now there was nothing sinister about the place; the lights blazed brightly and the muted music reached them, for the fiesta was still in full swing.

Rowdy's face softened with many remembrances; this was the lot of the fiddle-footed, to tarry briefly on a range and then to ride over the hill, but a man had a right to his own fleeting regrets. Then he said, "It's so long, Stumpy, to some new friends. We leave this a more peaceable place than we found it. That's better pay than the cash we tote with us. What do you think?"

But that lonesome lamb, Stumpy, safely lashed in his saddle, had fallen asleep, and only his snores, suddenly clamorous in the silence, gave answer to Rowdy.

We hope you have enjoyed this Large Print book. Other Thorndike Press or Chivers Press Large Print books are available at your library or directly from the publishers.

For more information about current and upcoming titles, please call or write, without obligation, to:

Thorndike Press
P.O. Box 159
Thorndike, Maine 04986 USA
Tel. (800) 223-2336

OR

Chivers Press Limited
Windsor Bridge Road
Bath BA2 3AX
England
Tel. (0225) 335336

All our Large Print titles are designed for easy reading, and all our books are made to last.